BECAUSE HE'S
WATCHING
KIRSTEN MCCURRAN

APRHODITE OMNIMEDIA

ALSO BY KIRSTEN MCCURRAN

Emma's Escape

Blank Canvas

The Wedding Party

Devil's Bargain

Sydney's Sin

Truth or Treat

Bound By Two

The Coach's Wife

Flirting With Trouble

Swinging Saved Our Marriage

Substitute Wife

Swapping Around the Christmas Tree

Sex Equity

Stormbound: Seduced by the Neighbors

Because He's Watching

Her Other Husband Series

A Snap Decision

Kissing In a Tree

Kelly Crosses the Line

Kelly Can't Help It

Kelly's Last Date

Eve & Friends Series

It Started With a Joke

It Started With Mistletoe

It Started Over Coffee

It Ended With an Announcement

BECAUSE HE'S WATCHING

Excerpt from *Because He's Watching: Ian's Obsession* ©2013 KW Publishing. Used with permission.

This is a work of fiction. All characters are fictitious or used fictitiously.

First Print Edition published by Aphrodite Omnimedia, January 2014
First Edition electronically published by Aphrodite Omnimedia, August 2011
Second Edition electronically published by Aphrodite Omnimedia, January 2014

Cover Design: Kenny Wright. Image licensed from bigstockphoto.com.

ISBN: 978-0615952468

FORWARD

Simply stated, I wouldn't be the author I am today were it not for Kirsten. Hell, I might not even be an author beyond the occasional hobbyist story on Literotica. Let me tell you a tale about two authors and a little story that could (but almost could not).

I had this idea for a story about a man who runs into a coworker of his wife's and learns that the guy has the hots for her. That was pretty much the entirety of it at the time. I started writing it, the idea took shape. Started branching. This guy—let's call him Ian, although I think he may have gone by something else at the time—becomes obsessed with what other men think of his wife. It triggers a deeply buried fantasy of his to watch her with other men.

But I needed another perspective on it. I wasn't crazy about where the story was going and needed some guidance. In steps Kirsten, who'd become a friend and sounding board by this time. Not only did she like the story idea, but she was intrigued enough by Ian's wife, Emily, that she wanted to explore what made Emily tick. I encouraged her to write a couple parallel chapters from Emily's perspective (mine was all from Ian's). I think Kirsten only intended to do a couple, more as a writing exercise than anything else. One chapter became two, became four, became ten. And now you've got the results of that "writing exercise" in your hand.

Oh, it wasn't all roses and sunshine. We disagreed on a few fundamentals, like what Ian's obsession-driven actions would do to a marriage. Looking back on it, the heated discussions helped produce a complex and realistic portrayal of what wife-watching and a hot-wife phenomenon can do to not only a marriage, but the individuals within the marriage. I was just stuck not liking my hero and not comfortable publishing a book about a guy like that. The plan had been to release the books at the same time, Tarantino-style.

Instead, Kirsten published Emily's story and I put Ian on ice. It was awesome to watch the success of *Because He's Watching*, but not encouraging enough for me to pull the trigger and publish *Ian's Obsession*. No, that took over two years, a lot of support from Kirsten, and a decent amount of maturing on my part.

What the success of this book did, though, was show me that people really were interested in this couple's story—a story that began with such a simple premise and grew into the clusterfuck of emotion that it is.

I wouldn't be the author I am today without Kirsten. *Because He's Watching* and *Ian's Obsession* is just one example. She's helped me as a collaborator, a beta reader, an editor, and most importantly of all, as a friend.

(And sorry guys and girls, but that's all she's been!)

Thanks, Kirsten!

Kenny Wright, December 2013

ONE

LOOKING BACK NOW, I think I can pinpoint the moment when my marriage really changed. At the time, I didn't think anything of it. Ian, my husband, came home late one evening after a particularly tough day at work. His team had blown a meeting and—feeling sorry for himself—he'd gone out drinking afterward. I love my husband dearly, but sometimes I wish he had more confidence. He's a good man, a good father to our two kids, but sometimes I feel like he doesn't know how much I appreciate him, although I try to tell him every day.

At first, I was just angry that he'd driven drunk, but he started coming on to me—not unusual when he drinks, and he melted my defenses. Like I said, I still love Ian as much as I ever have and I still find him sexy after twelve years of marriage. He was the first man I really felt I could be myself with and let all my barriers down. I don't think enough women take that into account when picking a guy. Ian's handsome, tall and slender with dark hair, but maybe not as much of it now that he's in his early forties, but do any of us look like we did when we were twenty-five? I go to the gym almost every day, but when I look in the mirror I still only see what I'd like to fix, not what I've achieved. So Ian may not be the hottest guy on the planet, but he'll always be the sexiest guy to me.

Ian kissed me with a passion I had not felt in a long, long time and it took my breath away. I ignored the beer on his breath and pressed my body to his and felt he was already getting hard. His unusual spontaneity was hot and, before I knew it, I was leading him to the bedroom. Luckily, I'd just put the kids down. We were barely in the bedroom when he slipped his hand into the back of my boy shorts and groped my ass. I giggled and let him enjoy himself. I'd put a lot of work into that butt and I was glad he appreciated it. I said his name as I turned around and melted into his arms for another hot kiss, my tongue slipping into his mouth. Ian's desire was heating me up very quickly.

I was already dressed for bed, so I didn't have much to strip off. I peeled my snug cami away and I'd barely thrown it onto the bed before Ian was grabbing me. He massaged my breasts, easily bringing my long nipples to taut stiffness. It was weird, but it felt like he was touching me for the first time, like he couldn't get enough of me. I didn't know where this new eagerness came from, but I liked it.

After I shimmied out of my boy shorts, Ian eased me backward and I sat on the edge of the bed while he went to his knees. He kissed my breasts all over, like he was trying to kiss each of the tiny freckles that dotted my chest. My breasts are not huge, they're full B's, but I'm proud that they are still perky and draw attention, even at my age. I've caught the guys at the office checking them out when they think I'm not looking. As long as they behave, I don't mind the attention. I can admit it, part of me even likes it. Those guys would love to see me the way Ian was at that moment. I'm not the kind of woman who likes to show off, but the thought gave me the shivers, especially when combined with the way Ian was kissing and sucking my breasts. My nipples are so sensitive, and he knows just how to touch me to get me warm and moaning. But he was only teasing. Once I whimpered his name, he started kissing down my belly and pushed me onto my back.

"Oooo…yesss…" I moaned when he kissed my pussy. I propped

up on my elbows so I could watch him and there was this incredible fire in his eyes. That was the first time I noticed something really different about my husband. Ian had me so wet, and when he pushed two fingers into me I cried out. His tongue moved rapidly and as he curved those fingers to hit my g-spot, he had me cumming easily. "AH! AH!" I cried out before remembering the kids and biting my lip to quiet down.

I was panting as Ian kissed his way up my body and I spread my legs for him. I don't know when he lost his pants, but he pushed inside me and I cried out as he filled me. He took me quickly, with strong thrusts, filling me completely and I closed my eyes, sinking into the wonderful sensations of our love making.

"Let's turn," Ian whispered to me.

It felt good and I didn't want him to stop. I groaned when he pulled out of me and we both moved up on the bed. This was new. We did not usually switch positions in the middle. But as I took him back inside me I didn't mind the interruption anymore. I love to be on top, because I can control everything and make sure I get my climax, even draw it out if I want to. And besides, I get the added benefit of Ian playing with me while I ride him. He kneaded my breasts as I rode him and he looked up at me lustily and I would have loved to have known what was going through his head.

"Oh, Ian…" I sighed when he leaned forward and kissed my breast. He hungrily sucked my nipple between his lips then chased it with his tongue, sending a charge through me, right down to my pussy. I fell forward, holding his head to my chest as my pussy clenched around him and my grip tightened and I rode him harder. He sucked on my other nipple and my breathing grew heavier as I gasped with pleasure and whimpered his name.

I pulled Ian into a hard kiss to muffle my growing moans. He grabbed my butt and pulled me into him and the bed creaked beneath us as we slammed together. We worked up a sweat and my nipples slid along his slick chest, the simple touch making me crazy. I was getting close, so close. Ian found the sweet spot on my neck and nibbled. It was like he was devouring me and I cried out, my entire body tightening as my orgasm was just on the horizon now. I pushed him away and arched my back, slamming my pussy onto him and ran my fingers through my long, dark, sweat-slick hair.

"Uhhh…Ian…Ian…" I cried as my world tilted like a ship on rough seas. I came so hard and I wanted Ian to cum with me. "Cum, Ian! Cum now, please!" I demanded. He exploded inside me and my muscles drained every last drop from him.

I rolled off of Ian and lay on my back, staring at the ceiling. Wow! That had been amazing! I turned to tell him so, but my husband—exhausted from our lovemaking, and all the beer he'd had—was already falling asleep. I just smiled and shook my head and then padded into the bathroom to clean up. Something had gotten into Ian that night, but I had no idea what. I would have thought he'd visited a strip club, if he was that kind of guy. Whatever it was, I couldn't complain. But little did I know that it was the beginning of a huge change in our marriage.

***

After that intense night of sex, things returned to normal for a few days. I could tell Ian was looking at me differently, but he didn't say anything about it. I figured it was just a phase and tried to ignore it. With two kids to take care of and a full plate at work, I just didn't have time to worry about what was going on in my husband's head.

Ian wasn't the only one acting differently. Ray, one of my coworkers, was suddenly paying me more attention as well. It was the oddest thing. I felt like my breasts had grown two sizes. I know I had an extra bounce in my step the morning after that hot night with Ian. Ray seemed to notice something different about me right away.

"Looks like someone got lucky last night," he joked when we met by the coffee machine.

"Maybe," I smiled knowingly.

I wasn't offended by his comment. We'd had a pretty flirty relationship from the time he started at the company, about a year ago. It was nice, to have a handsome younger man show an interest, even if it just was harmless fun. I've never been the woman that guys like Ray take an interest in. Those guys always go for the flashy blonde, with the big chest. That is certainly not me. I've always been the "cute" one, the girl guys want to take home to their mother, not the one they want to get down and dirty with. My thick, dark hair falls past my shoulders and a light dusting of freckles dapples my cheeks. People look at me and just think I'm the innocent, good girl. I'm petite, and going to the gym keeps my figure tight. I've been told more than once that I look younger than the thirty-six I am. But it's not in me to flaunt what I've got, not too much anyway. The sexy little things I do, I do for myself and sometimes I fantasize about being that bad girl no one expects. Only Ian knows that side of me.

Ray was about ten years or so younger than me, and built in a way that gets women mentally undressing a man. I could tell right away by how his shirts stretched over his broad chest and how his slacks hugged his butt that this man took care of himself. That was confirmed when I started seeing him at the same gym I attended during my lunch hour. So if this handsome, young hunk wanted to flirt with me, who was I to stop him?

"Really? There's still some fire left in the old furnace?" He sounded surprised.

"What do you mean?"

"Just you don't see women who've been married as long as you come into work smiling like you are."

I laughed. "Not all marriages turn into monotony and boredom, Ray." Although I had to admit, before that night things had gotten somewhat routine. "And besides, there are plenty of things about me that would surprise you, dear."

"Oh, I'm sure," he replied and I'm sure he was checking out my butt as I left the break room.

It wasn't the first time I caught him sneaking a peek, but it was the first time he was so open about it. I flushed, but smiled and hoped he enjoyed the view. The gray slacks I wore really did show off my butt. The rest of that day Ray found more excuses than usual to come around my cubicle and talk and he made a few more comments about how I must be bored after being with the same man for so long. I assured him that I loved my husband, but that didn't mean I never had other thoughts.

"I mean, I'm not dead, right? Ian is a wonderful and loving husband, but girls like to look around just like guys do. Sometimes I'll see a hot young guy and have a thought or two." I couldn't believe I was telling him that, but he had worn me down throughout the day.

"You've got to tell me more, Emily."

"I don't have to do anything of the kind, Ray. And you'd better get back to work before someone notices you're not doing anything. Just use your imagination." God only knows what he was imagining, but a huge smile spread across his face. I knew that handsome, charming smile well and, I'll admit, it made my heart skip a beat knowing he might be thinking something dirty about me. Is it awful that I was teasing him like that? I don't think so.

***

A couple days later, everyone was headed out for Happy Hour after work and Ray insisted I join them. It was not a surprise. He'd kept up his extra attention for the past few days, coming on strong. I tried to explain I had to get home to take care of the kids, but he wouldn't take no for an answer. He was like the Pied Piper and I couldn't resist his tune. Deciding there was no harm in one drink, I left Ian a message and let him know I would be late and said not to hold dinner. Besides, I hadn't gone out with the guys from work in ages, I told myself. It had *nothing* to do with Ray's insistence.

It was nice to be out with everyone and have a couple glasses of wine. Sometimes, you just need to feel like an adult in your own right, not someone's wife, someone's mother. I hope that doesn't sound terrible, but sometimes you need some time for yourself. We hit one of the usual haunts, an Irish pub called McGinty's. It was large, but felt intimate because of all the dark wood and brass rails and red upholstery. The place was crowded with a lot of hedge fund and banking types when we arrived, but the six of us found a corner for ourselves at the end of the bar. I ordered a glass of merlot, which brought ribbing from the others, who were all guys. They treated me like an equal, which made me proud since the office was quite the boys' club. I'm the only woman in our department who's not an administrative assistant.

The crowd made it hot in the bar and I slipped off my jacket, putting it over the back of my stool, and opened an extra button on my blouse. I didn't realize how much that exposed me until I caught Ray looking down my blouse when I leaned forward to pick up my glass. With the way Ray had been behaving the last couple days I had to resist the urge to pull my blouse closed—I didn't want to give him any real encouragement. But then, it would be obvious I knew he was looking if I just buttoned it back up, I told myself. And if I'm honest, I liked the way he had been looking at me the past couple days. If a hot younger guy like Ray was showing so much interest then I must still have it.

I probably shouldn't have hit the wine like that after having such a light lunch, because naughty thoughts crept into my head. *Just how much could he see*, I wondered. Could he see the lacy edge of my black Victoria's Secret bra? Did he like the cleavage it created? And is it bad that I wanted him to? It was just harmless fun, right? That's what I told myself, anyway.

Sexy lingerie is something I'd started indulging in over the past few years. When I got back into shape after having our son Davy, I wanted to do something to show how good I felt about myself. It makes me feel sexy to wear something silky and frilly underneath the business clothes I have to wear for work every day. It's like a secret I have that all those guys around me have no idea about. The lightly-padded bras give me a little boost, and hide my sensitive nipples, and the thigh-highs I've taken to wearing just make me feel naughty. If only those guys knew! Sometimes, I wished Ian took more notice of it, especially the thigh-highs. He always used to try to talk me into wearing them, but I just felt silly. Now that I'm little older and more confident I like it and don't care if it's not practical. Unfortunately, my husband takes less notice of such things now that we've been married for so long. I don't think he ever notices what I wear to work, which is when I am the most dressed-up.

As we talked, I noticed a couple of the other guys were sneaking peeks too, and I've got to say, it had an effect on me. I might have even leaned forward more than I needed to. As long as I pretended not to notice, there was no awkwardness. I blamed my feelings on

Ray's heightened attention. I sat on one of the high stools with my legs crossed and he stood behind me, over my right shoulder. He kept putting his hands on my arms and pressing against me when he leaned in to grab his beer from the bar and I started to get worried that the others might notice. The last thing I wanted was to put an idea into those guys' perverted heads, but I was trapped and didn't have much of a choice. At the end of my second glass of wine, I wasn't as worried about it and just enjoyed it.

The others filtered out until it was just me and Ray. He sat next to me with his hand on mine as it rested on the bar. As we talked, he kept glancing down and I blushed furiously when I realized he could see the lacy top of my stocking. I wore a snug pencil skirt that came to the knee, which was safe, but it had a small slit on the side. The way I sat with my legs crossed had pulled it open. I didn't even want to know what he was thinking now.

"It's good to have you out with us," Ray said. "We don't see much of you."

"It's tough to balance having two kids with having a real life. It's like my real work begins when I get home at night. Work is almost a break." I laughed.

"But you do need some time to enjoy yourself. Do you and uhh…"

"Ian." Did he intentionally forget my husband's name?

"Ian, right. Do you and Ian ever get out for date night?"

"Not often, but we have plenty of time for ourselves. Don't worry about us."

"On Demand movies on the couch. Exciting!" Ray teased.

"It gets more exciting than that. Don't you think married people have sex?"

"In the beginning, sure, but it falls off over time. I've got to be honest, I know that I'm not ready to swear that I'll only ever have sex with one person for the rest of my life."

"I'm not going to give you details, but Ian and I have a great sex life. And if you love someone then they are all you need," I answered. "I guess you haven't truly been in love yet."

Ray laughed. "Maybe, maybe not. All I am saying is that forever is a long time, and when someone is still young and hot like you, well, sometimes it's got to be hard for you to walk the straight-and-narrow."

"Ray! Stop it!" I chided. It was the first time he'd ever come right out and said he thinks I'm hot. I must have turned three shades of red.

"A beautiful woman like you should be used to taking compliments." He squeezed my hand, then nodded toward my empty glass. "Would you like another?"

The last glass of wine had been my third and I had a buzz on, so yet another one was not a good idea. I checked my watch and couldn't believe how late it was. Ian must have been ready to send out a search party.

"I really need to get going. The trains only run every hour this late, and I've got a walk to the station from here."

"Don't be silly. I'll drive you home."

"Ray, it's too far," I protested. "It's got to be a least a half hour drive each way. I can't ask you to do that." I knew he had a condo in the city.

"You're not asking. I want to, and I don't take no for an answer."

He paid the bill and pulled the stool away from the bar so I could hop down. I took my purse and jacket, but left the latter off because it was a warm evening. He took my arm in his during the walk back to the parking garage, a very gentlemanly, even romantic, gesture. Ray was so solid. It was the first time I'd ever actually touched him, except to shake hands, and his arm was like stone. It was like being walked down the street by some Greek sculpture. Except Ray was clothed, I thought naughtily. I leaned into him as we walked, enjoying his strength.

Ray held the door of his expensive, black Mercedes coupe and I felt quite elegant as I slid into the buttery-soft leather seat. I know he got both a glimpse down my blouse and at my stocking top, but by that point, I didn't mind. All that wine, combined with being out with a handsome young man, had taken a toll. I was very horny and couldn't wait to get home to Ian. He was in for quite a treat. It would be my way of paying him back for when he came home all sexed up the other night.

The expensive black sports car made easy work of the roads, gliding in an out of traffic. Ray worked the six-speed transmission like a master and squeezed every ounce of power out of the softly purring engine. He controlled the sleek vehicle so easily that I couldn't help but think of how easily he could take control in other areas.

I told Ray he only had to run me to the train station because I'd left the car there, but he wanted to take me home. He said he wasn't sure I should be driving, but I felt fine by the time we were back out in the suburbs. He kept checking me out in the darkened car, and I think he just wanted to keep me with him a little longer. He wasn't the only one. I kept looking over through the shifting shadows and watched his strong jaw and those stormy eyes. It was like I was in the car with my very own action hero.

It might have been a sudden attack of conscious for the heavy flirting I'd been doing all night. That, and I didn't know how my husband would feel if he saw I was being dropped off at home by another man, so when we turned onto my street, I asked Ray to stop a few houses down from ours.

"Tonight was great. You really need to come out more," Ray said, setting the parking brake.

"It was fun. I'll definitely come out whenever I can get away." Just thinking about going home to all that chaos my kids create put a damper on me. Sitting in that car with Ray, I was an exotic, dangerous woman. Back in the house, I was mom.

"Don't wait too long. You know I won't be around much longer and you'll miss me when I'm gone." There was that smile again.

"Maybe," I replied coyly and unlocked the seatbelt.

I leaned over to kiss Ray on the cheek, but he caught me and guided my lips to his. I was so stunned that I did nothing at first. But he held me there, fingers tousling my hair, and his lips were so insistent that I weakened and kissed him back. We probably only kissed for a handful of seconds, but it felt like forever. Suddenly the car was so hot I could hardly stand it. Ray's lips were soft, but there was a power there and I would have gone weak in the knees if I hadn't been sitting. Only when I felt his tongue slipping between my lips did I come to my senses. He let me pull away and I fell back into my seat, breathless.

"Ray! I'm married! Why did you…" I stammered, gathering my things and reaching for the door latch.

"I'm sorry, Emily. I couldn't help myself, and I thought I was picking up signals."

"I was not sending you any signals!"

"Emily…"

"Listen, I've got to go. My husband and kids are waiting for me."

I swung out of the car, slammed the door, and immediately saw Ian and the kids in front of the house. It looked like they were just coming home. I plastered a smile on my face and waved to Ray as he drove away. I didn't want Ian thinking anything was amiss. But beneath that smile, I was a mess. God, how was I going to face Ray in the office? How the hell had that happened?

It only took the short walk to the front door for my outrage to wear off and my smile to become genuine. Maybe I had sent out some mixed signals, but I blamed it on the wine. And what a kiss! It was so hot! Ray said, *he couldn't help himself!* A guy like him wanted to kiss me, and couldn't help himself! By the time I reached my family I was glowing and thinking I couldn't get Ian alone fast enough.

"Mommy," Jenny shouted, as she charged into my arms. I scooped her up and walked over to Ian, who had the oddest look on his face. It was like he'd just eaten something bad. I kissed him longer and with more passion than I usually would in front of the kids.

"How's my favorite family?" I asked.

Ian didn't answer and storm clouds crossed his face when I bent down to put Jenny on the ground. I was sure he looked down my blouse and I thought I must be sexy if even my husband is checking me out like that. Still, he had that strange look, and for the first time in our marriage I couldn't tell what he was thinking. Did he see Ray as he drove away and was angry? Why would he be? Ian couldn't have seen Ray make the pass at me, and even if he had, he's not usually the jealous type. Actually, he's proven to be the opposite over the years. I was just projecting my own guilt onto him, I decided. Or maybe not.

"Who dropped you off, hon?" Ian asked, pointedly nonchalant.

"Just a co-worker," I said, and felt my pale cheeks flushing. "I had one glass of wine too many, so he did me a favor."

"Anyone I know?" he asked, smiling.

"I'm not sure. I don't think you and Ray have met." I felt guilty just saying the name, and I realized that his mouth may have been smiling, but his eyes were blank.

"He's quite a gentleman, offering to drop you off," Ian replied, putting his arm around me while we walked. His smile did not reach his eyes.

"You're not jealous, are you?" I met his eyes for the first time and felt like he could see right through me.

I didn't know what to say, so I replied, "To be continued," and busied myself with the children.

Ian watched me closely as I went about putting the kids to bed. Was he looking for something specific? Did he see Ray kiss me and think I did something to encourage it? I might have, but at that moment, I wasn't ready to be that honest with myself. Ray and I had always flirted, and I don't know that I did anything tonight to make him think it was okay to kiss me.

"What?" I finally asked, bent over to put the diaper bag away.

"Watching you in that outfit, I'm beginning to wish I worked with you."

"Really?" I replied, relieved that he wasn't jealous. He was horny. Whatever had a hold of him the other night must have come back. I laughed. "You letch. Do I need to file a sexual harassment complaint?"

Ian pulled me to my feet and into his arms. "You'd be complaining, would you?"

"You're pretty sure of yourself," I smiled.

He responded by pulling me tighter, so I could feel his hard-on through his pants.

"Yeah, this is definitely sexual harassment," I giggled.

"Oh, come on. Don't tell me guys haven't ever come onto you. I'm sure that guy Ray and you have flirted a little."

Was Ian psychic? I was worried for a second, but from his smile and his erection, I knew that he wasn't angry and jealous. It slowly dawned on me. Ian was turned on by seeing another man drop me off at home. He thought I looked sexy, and he liked that maybe the guys around my office thought so too. I was shocked, but I shouldn't have been. After what happened last year, it's not like it was without precedent.

"Maybe… I think we should discuss this in my office," I replied and smiled slyly.

The bedroom door was barely closed before Ian was on top of me. I attacked him just as ferociously, pulling at his shirt while he fumbled with the buttons on my blouse.

"Uhhh…honey…it feels so good…" I whimpered as I pulled his cock out of his jeans.

Our legs tangled and we tumbled onto the bed together, groping and furiously kissing each other. All of that sexual tension with Ray came bubbling to the surface. I couldn't remember the last time I wanted Ian so badly. I was already soaked down below and couldn't wait to get him inside me. Was it terrible that another man's attention had me dying to make love to my husband?

He hiked up my skirt, almost tearing it at the slit, and wrenched my thong to the side. He rammed his cock in me and I gasped at the feeling of being instantly filled. He gripped my thigh, right over my stocking top, and took me forcefully. It was even more intense than the other night and I couldn't help but think of Ray. I know he's the type of man who takes his women. I could just imagine him hiking up my skirt and taking me the way that Ian was. I knotted my fingers in his hair, pulling, like I was pulling him into me. His weight pressed onto me, pinning me to the bed, and all of the sudden, I climaxed. I threw my body back at Ian's as the orgasm ripped through me.

"Do it, lover…do it…Ian…ahhh…"

I felt him cum inside me then fully collapse onto my body, burying his face in the spill of my dark hair. I loved this fiery, passionate version of my husband, but I was dying to know where it was coming from.

"What got into you?" I asked.

"Mm, maybe I should ask, what got into *you?*" He kept me pinned to the bed, our faces inches apart. "Your gentleman suitor maybe?"

"Ray? Ian, don't be silly…" I turned my face away from his, not wanting my hazel eyes to betray anything.

"It is!" Ian said, almost triumphantly.

Then I felt Ian stiffen inside me, and it cemented my thought before. The idea of me being attracted to another man excited my husband. I didn't know how to feel about that. Should I be angry? "Thinking about me and Ray turns you on, doesn't it?" I asked.

"Maybe a little. That's weird, isn't it?"

Instead of answering him, I followed my impulses and kissed Ian. It was a slow, sensual kiss that turned increasingly passionate and I felt him twitch inside me. Our tongues fought and he was fully hard again. That was impressive recovery time. He rolled off of me and his hard cock slipped out with a slurp. I missed him inside of me. I was as ready for round two as he was.

"Do you always dress like that for work?" Ian asked.

I looked back over my shoulder, thick, chestnut hair veiling my face as I stood. "Do you mean like this?" I asked. I pulled my skirt down and it smoothed across my butt as I bent forward to give him the best view. His eyes widened when I turned, giving him the same peek at my thigh-high that Ray got back in the bar. Did Ray like it as much as my husband did? The thought made me tingle all over.

"I think it would look even better like this," Ian said, and reached over to draw down the zipper over my butt. He winked and I wiggled, letting the skirt drop to the floor. I felt so sexy standing there in just my shirt and high heels, with my thigh-highs exposed. He ran his fingers over the exposed flesh above my stocking, making me quiver.

"This is just like Bobby's wedding, isn't it?" I asked in a breathy whisper. We'd never talked about that night, but that was why it wasn't such a shock that Ian was turned on by seeing Ray drop me off.

A year ago, we had attended the wedding of Ian's nephew. Ian had just injured his knee and was stuck at our table all night, sipping beers. Being the loving husband he is, he encouraged me to dance with others because I love to dance. At first I said no, I would stick to his side, but he insisted, so when one of the groomsmen asked me, I joined him on the dance floor. He was a handsome younger man in his mid-twenties and a great dancer, but I felt guilty about dancing with him, so as soon as the song ended I returned to Ian to make sure he wasn't jealous. He insisted he wasn't and told me to go back out there and have fun. I ended up staying out there for much of the night, fueled by seemingly endless glasses of wine and the enthusiasm of all the younger men there. It was like I was passed from one handsome, younger man to another, to another, and to another. Soon, my head was spinning with mixed emotions. I enjoyed being in the arms of these fun guys. It took me back to a time when I was younger and single and carefree.

But as the night wore on, I danced with one of the guys more than the others. His name was Kyle, and he was tall and buff, very much like Ray, actually. He looked achingly handsome in his tuxedo, and it was exciting that he wanted to dance with me. I felt so sexy in his arms and, after stopping him the first few times, I eventually let his hands stray to my butt. I wasn't thinking about my husband as I laid my head on his broad chest and closed my eyes. I was thinking about how he would look out of that tux.

I only returned to Ian when the music ended, and I was sure he would be angry. But no. There was a fire in his eyes like I'd never seen before. We went back to our room and had the hottest sex since our honeymoon, and Ian watched me like I was a sex goddess as I rode him. I couldn't help but think that I wanted Kyle to look at me that way. It was the first time I wanted someone other than Ian to see my inner sex kitten. It was an incredible night, but we never did discuss why we were both so horny. I think we were both too embarrassed.

"Yeah. It turned you on too, didn't it?" Ian said.

"You know it did, but I was worried of what you thought of me." I was so aroused that night. I went on pure instinct, never pausing to think about what could happen.

"You didn't know? Can you read my mind now?"

I looked down at his raging hard-on as I peeled off my blouse. "I don't think I need to. But do I really want to know what you were thinking that night?"

Ian looked chagrined. "Probably not."

Half-turning, I unclasped my bra and tossed it on the bed and saw Ian was focused on my breasts. Sometimes I think he loves my chest the best. The erotic tension in the bedroom was electric.

"Does that guy who dropped you off ever flirt with you? I mean, you are a beautiful woman."

"A beautiful, *married* woman. But yes, sometimes we flirt. He's just one of those guys. Does it turn you on?" I cupped my breasts and shivered as I touched my nipples.

Ian pulled off his remaining clothes and watched me from the edge of the bed. "Maybe. Is it just flirting?"

"Do you want to know how serious it is?" I played with my thong as I spoke, watching him carefully. It was the first time we'd ever explored this, and I thought my heart was going to beat out of my chest. "Are you asking if it's more than just *harmless* flirting? Does

Ray ever push it?"

"Emily…" He looked anguished, but he was harder than ever.

"What do you want to know? Do you want to know if he makes passes at me?" I rolled down my thong and straddled him. I was so slick from our first quickie that he slid right into me. It felt so good.

"Does he?"

"Yes. He tried to kiss me tonight," I whispered. I could feel Ray's lips on mine again and I tightened around my husband.

"You knew he wanted you, and you let him drive you home." Ian gripped my hips and surged inside me.

"Yes. I'm a big girl, I can handle myself. Ohhh, Ian…" I started rocking back and forth on him.

"And he kissed you…"

"He tried, but I stopped him," I moaned. *After a moment*, I thought. We started moving faster and I thought about the hunger in Ray's kiss. I could feel how much he wanted me, the way Ian wanted me now. Somehow, Ray saw that side of me I reserve only for my husband. It excited *and* scared me.

I couldn't be sure, but it was almost like Ian breathed the word, *why*. He said, "I love you, Emily."

"I love you too, honey." A wave of guilt swamped me. How could I feel those things about Ray. It was so wrong! "I love you so much," I stressed.

"Show me," Ian moaned.

We consumed each other with a passion we rarely reached anymore. It was something we shared only when we'd been parted, or when we connected on a deep, deep level, which was so rare with the kids and our obligations. We made love with the intensity we did that night after Bobby's wedding, when I thought of Kyle and I know Ian was thinking of me *with* Kyle. We clawed at each other, lips smearing across each other as we each fought to control the kiss and our coupling. As I came into the home stretch, I pushed him onto his back and rode hard as he dug his fingers into my plush ass, pulling me into him. I slammed up and down on him and quickly reached a rare peak.

"Oh God! Oh God!" Ian cried underneath me as he came.

"Yes! Yes! Yes!" I breathed, oddly quiet as I came. I ran my fingers through his chest hair and then slumped forward. He buried his face in my breasts and we slowly came down from our high.

Later, when we lay in bed together, naked, Ian finally spoke.

"You know, I was thinking…"

"Don't hurt yourself," I laughed. It felt good to laugh. The tension was gone.

"I think we should meet up for Happy Hour sometime."

"Sure, it would be fun," I said.

"*And* maybe we could pretend to be strangers?" It was more question than statement. I know he was feeling me out.

"Pretend to be strangers? So you can come in and hit on me?" I couldn't suppress my giggles. My first thought was that he was being silly, but then I warmed to the idea. It could be fun. And maybe it was a way to explore this vague fantasy we both seemed to have.

"You think I'm crazy," he said, looking away.

I kissed him. "I'm game. When?"

Ian beamed. "How about Friday after work? I've heard good things about this place called Bar 88."

TWO

It turns out I didn't need to be so worried about seeing Ray in work the next morning. He was very good about the whole thing when I pulled him aside during our morning break. The smokers all went out one door and spent their break in a designated smoking area, while I asked Ray to meet me on the other side of the building. My tummy flip-flopped as I waited for him to come out and join me.

"Hey, Emily," Ray said, as the door closed behind him.

"Ray," I replied, staring at the ground.

I could feel him checking me out again, even though I'd purposely chosen an outfit that didn't quite hide my body, but didn't show it off either: a pair of slacks and a loose jacket over a light blue sweater. Trying to dress down that morning, I realized for the first time just how much I'd been dressing up. I really enjoyed the flirting and feeling sexy, and that was a relatively new thing for me. But I had never intended for it to go as far as it had last night. I'd had too much wine and just enjoyed myself too much.

"Listen," I started, still looking at the ground, "I don't know if I was sending out signals, or I gave you the wrong idea…"

"Emily…"

"Please, let me finish, or I'll never get this out. I know that we're always flirting and it's a lot of fun, I like it, but I never meant it as more than that. I like you, a lot, but just as a friend. I have a husband, who I love very much. If I did something last night because I had too much to drink, then I'm sorry." I took a deep breath, and finally looked him in the eye.

"Are you done?"

"I think so." I smiled weakly.

"I was going to say I'm sorry," he said. "Yes, I thought I was picking up a vibe. Somehow I got this crazy idea in my head that there was something else there. I'm not going to lie. You're hot as hell, Emily. Your husband is a lucky man. But you *do* have a husband and I shouldn't have made a pass at you. This hasn't ruined our friendship, has it?"

"No, of course not." I saw that smile and those dark eyes, and my mind went right back to that kiss. I could almost taste him on my lips. I was attracted to Ray in a deeply visceral way. It was something I couldn't control and I realized I was lying. It would be hard to just be friends with him.

"That's great."

Ray pulled me into a hug and I clung to him. Oddly, I thought of Ian. Was my attraction to Ray okay because it turned on my husband? If I told Ian that I wanted Ray to kiss me again, would it turn him on? It seemed that it would. I almost convinced myself that I could kiss Ray again and I'd be doing it for Ian. I stepped away from Ray.

"Then were all good?" I said.

"We're good."

Even though we were good, I'll admit I avoided him the rest of that week, hoping my ardor would cool. Instead, I focused on the game Ian and I would be playing Friday night, and how much fun we were going to have. We could indulge this newfound fantasy, but with each other. Knowing how Ian felt, I don't think he'd mind if I pretended he was Ray while we played.

Ian was excited too. We made love every night that week, but we did not speak of our plan. Keeping it under wraps until the night arrived seemed to make it just that much hotter. Ian was like a little kid waiting for Christmas. I could see it in the gleam in his eye and the way he carried himself. I don't think he'd been so excited for anything in a long time.

I brought another outfit to work with me, so I could be sexy for my "one night stand," and I made sure everyone was out of the office before I went into the ladies room to change and do my make-up. The last thing I wanted was for Ray to see me all made up for a "date."

Ian's parents had the kids, so we'd have all night. I couldn't believe how energized I was thinking about what might happen. My enthusiasm was only slightly dampened when I got a text from Ian saying he was running late. I texted back that he'd better not leave me waiting too long, or someone else might pick me up, and added a smiley face. I knew that would get his motor running.

Bar 88 was a nice place. It was just outside of downtown and not too close to the office, which made me feel better. I'd be horribly embarrassed if anyone we knew saw us playing our game. It was an old, re-done industrial space with an upscale ambiance, and the bar seemed to be filling quickly with young professionals a few years younger than Ian and I. The first floor was large and open, with a giant, rectangular bar and an open dance floor with a small stage for a band or a DJ. Beside that were some pool tables. A second floor loft had tables for dining. It reminded me of the places Ian and I went before we had kids.

I arranged myself on a barstool to my best effect, so I would catch Ian's eye as soon as he came in. I knew he would like all the effort I'd made because of the looks I was drawing from the men around me. I'd chosen a daring, chocolate-brown dress that hugged my butt, with a halter neckline that draped low in the front, showing off a lot of my perky breasts, which were free. I never go out braless, but I never show that much cleavage either. Tonight was a special night. The dress was very short, and barely hid my stocking tops. My hair was pulled up with glittery combs and my lips were painted red.

I ordered a glass of wine, hooked one of my three-inch stiletto heels on the stool, crossed my legs and waited.

After about ten minutes, I looked through the crowd and my heart almost stopped. I saw Ray at one of the pool tables. Had he been there all along, or had he just come in? How could I have missed him? I turned in to face the bar, hoping he wouldn't see me. How was it that of all the bars Ian and I could have met in, we'd chosen one that Ray frequented? I pulled out my phone and texted Ian, asking how long he'd be. After a few more minutes, Ian still hadn't replied, and I ordered a second glass of wine to steady my nerves.

Despite the wine, I was increasingly nervous. What would Ray think if he saw me like this? There was still no reply from Ian and almost forty-five minutes had passed. I turned around again and scanned the bar, looking for my husband, but there was no sign of him. I even looked upstairs, wondering if I'd misunderstood where we were supposed to meet.

There weren't a lot of people up there, but one guy sat at a table for two by the railing, trying very hard not to be noticed. He wore a baggy hoodie, a Yankees cap and thick-framed, black Buddy Holly glasses. It just screamed disguise. I looked more closely and with a shock I realized it was Ian. No, I had to be wrong, but I thought I recognized the hoodie, not that he often wears hooded sweatshirts. It just couldn't be him. I was seeing things because I was nervous. But then he looked away when he saw me looking up there and I was sure it was Ian. What the hell was he doing?

Did Ian want to play a different game than he proposed? I remember him watching me at that wedding. What turned him on was watching me flirt with other men. Is that what he wanted? He wanted to hide and watch me flirt with strange men at the bar? My heart beat faster just thinking about it. I was already turned on from the way the men around me were looking. I didn't know if I could do it, though. It felt creepy that Ian wanted to hide in the shadows and watch this, no matter how much it turned me on. It angered me. I felt set-up, and I was tempted to go upstairs and ream him out.

But then I thought the thing to do was to give him what he wanted and really play it up. That would teach him a lesson about putting me out there like bait.

Then I remembered Ray. I couldn't do this with *him* there. For a paranoid second, I thought Ian must have somehow known Ray would be there. That really would be the perfect set-up for my husband. Not only would I be flirting with other men, but I'd be flirting with the hunky co-worker that had Ian all fired up. Ian could not have planned it better. But that was crazy—Ian didn't know Ray. They'd only met briefly at a work function months ago. There was no way he could know Ray would be here.

Suddenly, I couldn't get Ray off my mind. If I did flirt with Ray that would *really* teach Ian a lesson. It would be more dangerous and shocking. I bet Ian would cum in his pants. But would Ian recognize Ray and know that's who I was flirting with? Probably not. Ian wouldn't get the full effect until I told him later when we were at home. If I hadn't already been well into my second glass of wine, I never would have entertained the idea. But I was so angry with Ian, and honestly, very horny, that I just went for it. I drained my glass, ordered another, and sauntered over to where Ray was shooting pool—

almost directly under Ian's perch in the loft.

"Hey there, stranger," I said with a smile.

Ray didn't recognize me at first, then did a double take while he drank me in. "Emily? What are you doing here?"

"I am meeting my husband for drinks, but apparently he's tied up, so I thought you might keep me company. Do you mind if I watch you play?"

"Hey, his loss is my gain." There was that smile again.

I sat on a stool by the wall behind him, knowing every time he turned around he'd have a great view of my legs. The hem of my dress just barely concealed my lacy stocking tops. I sat my drink and clutch down on the little round table beside me and took out my phone. I wanted to be sure I would see it when Ian chickened out and texted me with a message to stop.

"Do you hang out here a lot?" Ray asked. "It's hardly in your neck of the woods." He went around the table to make a shot and tried very hard to check me out nonchalantly, but he didn't do it well.

"No. Meeting here was Ian's idea actually. I guess it's just my good luck that I ran into you, or I'd be at the mercy of all the men in here."

"Looking like that, they'd eat you alive," he joked. His snug V-neck really brought out his eyes and showed off his muscles. The expensive jeans hugged that hard ass every time he bent over to take a shot.

"Oh, this?" I asked with mock sincerity. "Do you like it? I bought it especially for tonight." I made sure to say *tonight* instead of *for my husband*.

"You don't want to know what I'm thinking, Emily. Let's just say you look very nice."

I turned almost as red as my lips and sipped my wine to cover it. Knowing Ray wanted me just made me want to vamp it up more. That's terrible I know, but I was enjoying myself. "Why don't you have a date tonight?"

"Maybe I came here hoping to get lucky."

Just as I was about to answer him, my phone buzzed with a text from Ian. He claimed he was going to be hung up even longer than he thought, and that we should reschedule. Yeah, right. I didn't even bother to text him back, since I knew he was watching anyway.

"Looks like it is your lucky night. That was Ian and he can't make it."

"You're not going home?" Ray sounded surprised.

"I am all ready to have fun tonight. The kids are with their grandparents, so I'm not going home."

Ray took a shot and missed and asked, "Do you play pool?"

"It's been a long time," I said, demurely.

"Show me what you've got," he replied, holding out the cue.

I'm afraid that's exactly what I did. I hopped off the stool, giving a little bounce to my breasts that would have revealed I was braless if he was really paying attention. When I bent over to take my shot, he stood behind me, and my dress rode up to completely reveal my stocking tops. Did I mention before that it hugged my ass. Also, Ian must have been looking right down the front of my dress from the balcony. I missed my shot, but I didn't much care. Ray took the cue and we settled into the rhythm of the game. When he took his shots, I leaned forward on the edge of the table to give him a perfect look down my dress, and he had to see how hard my long nipples were through the fabric. The flirting got hot and heavy and I was getting so aroused. I really did feel like a sexy, single woman out to pick up a handsome guy. I kept stealing looks up at Ian in the balcony, but rather than steady me, that only made me hornier. Showing off for my husband was such a turn-on, and I leaned over the table once more.

"Here, let me show you. You'll never make the shot that way," Ray said.

He came around and pressed in behind me. The contact with his hard body took my breath away. He bent me forward over the table to position me and I felt his hot breath on my neck as his fingers glided down my arm. I shivered. I imagined Ray just hiking up my dress and taking me from behind in the middle of the bar while my husband watched. I felt weak, and I thought that if I could find a way to grind into one corner of the pool table, I might cum. What was Ian thinking while he watched this? He hadn't put a stop to it. How far did he want me to go? It was time to find out.

I told myself this was all about teaching Ian a lesson, but truth is, I just really wanted it. I turned around and our eyes locked. I laughed nervously when Ray brushed a stray lock of hair back from my cheek and a breath caught in my throat when Ray leaned in. He was waiting for me to make the move. *Watch this, Ian!* I thought. I did not hesitate this time. Not for a second. Ray's lips were hot and soft, but the kiss was firm and fiery. His strong hand massaged the back of my neck, under my hair. If we were in private, he so easily could have unsnapped my halter. I slipped him my tongue and he lightly sucked it. I held Ray tightly to me and enjoyed a long, passionate kiss. When it ended, we both giggled, but stayed pressed together.

"Ray…"

"You're not going to tell me you didn't want that," he answered. His hand slid down to my bare back, still caressing. I melted.

"No, I did. I don't know what to say."

"Then don't say anything at all."

We kissed again, I don't know who started it, but I gave myself to him completely. My arms went around him and I thought I felt a bulge in the front of his jeans as he pulled me tight. I was leaning against the pool table, so I couldn't have escaped if I'd wanted to, but I didn't. I couldn't I believe my husband was watching this, and that I was doing this in public at all. It was like we were horny teenagers. He lightly rubbed my ass and I let him.

I slipped away from Ray and reached for the wineglass I had left at our table nearby, still well within Ian's view, but facing away from the, bar, near a wall where no one could really see us.. I downed the rest of it in one gulp. My head was spinning. What was I doing? There was no text from Ian, no warning to stop. Ray came up behind me, held me, and kissed my neck. I leaned my head back on his chest, letting him support me.

"You are so goddammed sexy, Emily. You have no idea how many times I've thought about this," he breathed.

"Oh, Ray…"

"I knew this was the real you, baby." He cooed. Was it?

Ray cupped my breasts from beneath and rolled my nipples. I shuddered and moaned, knowing I should stop him. From his perch, I was sure all Ian could see was that Ray was holding me from behind and kissing my neck, though he might have guessed at what was going on. It felt so good. I was so wet and close to losing control. Again, I wondered just how far Ian wanted to take this. Did he really want to leave me to the mercies of another man?

I gathered myself and turned away. There was no one in the balcony. Our watcher was gone. I panicked. Even if Ian was angry, he wouldn't have just left, would he? Oh my God. What had I done? I was fooling around on my husband. I felt faint and had to lean into Ray.

"Are you alright?" he asked.

"I am. I just need some air," I lied. I just had to get out of there.

I told Ray to let me go outside, but he wouldn't just do that. He walked me out to the parking lot and we ended up standing by his car, with him behind me rubbing my shoulders. I had never been so conflicted in my life. I knew I had to leave. I had to get out of there, but I loved his hands on my shoulders, and I couldn't make myself pull away from him. He drew me closer, his arms around my waist again and his lips were on my neck.

"Ray…" I breathed. I meant to tell him to stop, but those words didn't come. Instead, I pressed my butt back into him and laced my fingers through his. I turned and he backed me against the car. We kissed again and his hands roamed my body. He started hiking up my dress, but I stopped him. Then he touched my breasts again, and I couldn't resist. When he thumbed my nipples, waves of pleasure went straight to my pussy. His hard cock pressed into me and I rubbed back against him. It was only when I realized Ray was not going to stop trying to pull up my dress that I pushed him back.

"We can't do this in public," I panted. I didn't tell him we couldn't do it because I was married.

"I don't live too far from here," he offered, looking like he would have taken me right on the hood of my car if I let him.

Stepping away from Ray, I took out my phone and found a message from Ian that he was wrapping up his work. I dialed his office. *Please don't be there*, I thought. I desperately wanted to believe he was lurking in the shadows somewhere, watching us.

"Hey, honey," Ian answered. He *was* at the office. I thought I was going to be sick. "Did you just leave the bar and go home? I'm really sorry about tonight."

"You're really at work?" I couldn't keep the surprise out of my voice.

"I'm on my way out the door now. It doesn't sound like you're at home. Did you really let some guy pick you up?" He was playing on my earlier joke, but I heard the excitement in his voice. Even if he wasn't here watching, he liked the idea of me flirting with other men at the bar.

"What do you think?" I snapped as my guilt flashed to anger. Even if I was wrong, Ian set this whole thing into motion. And if I told him I'd hooked up with Ray would it turn him on even more? "Don't rush things at the office. We're not done yet. I'll see you at home." I cut the connection.

Ray was still waiting by his car and I felt like the world's worst cock tease. I pulled him to me and kissed him hard. "Could you give me a ride to the train station to get my car? I really should be getting home."

"Sure."

When he wasn't working the gearshift, Ray rested his hand on my thigh, fingering the top of my stocking and my garter strap. I usually just go for stand-up stockings, but I knew Ian would think the garter belt was hot. Now Ray was enjoying it. I sat back and closed my eyes, thinking about how that hand would feel other places. The way I sank back into the car seat my dress seemed impossibly short. We pulled into the parking lot and mine was one of the few cars still there.

"Thanks for the ride. This is becoming a habit," I smiled.

"I just wish I was driving you back to my place."

"You know I can't do that, Ray. I did have a great time tonight, though."

"Maybe we'll do it again," he said hopefully.

"You never know."

Ray leaned over the center console when he kissed me and I pressed into him. My fingers raked through his thick, dark hair and his hands explored my curves, mapping the swell of my breasts until I moaned into our kiss. Then caressing my legs, he pressed up into the humid darkness under my dress. I stopped him at first, but I was weak and my legs slightly parted. My thong was soaked, stuck to my pussy and when he pressed I swooned until I regained control and pulled his hand away again.

"Goodnight," I told him, and exited the car on unsteady feet.

***

I beat Ian home, went upstairs to change and almost masturbated. I don't do that often, but I was so horny I could hardly stand it. Instead, I changed into my robe and scrubbed my make-up off. I set my hair in a ponytail. When I finished, I sat in the dark living room and waited for my husband.

"Welcome home, Ian," I called out when I heard him come through the door. It was late. Later than it should have been if he'd come straight home.

"You're home." It was his turn to sound surprised. "You… on the phone… I thought you were still out…"

I sat on the armrest of the couch. "Out with some stranger? Is that what you wanted? Was that really your game?" I struggled to keep my voice neutral.

"I'm sorry I got hung up at work." He was worried. I know that man.

"I thought you were there. I thought you were watching me." A quiver in my voice.

"I'm sorry," he said, confused.

"You have no idea."

I didn't know whether to punch him or breakdown crying and

apologize. Strangely, I crossed the room and kissed his neck softly. I was angry and there were so many things I needed to say, but none of that mattered at that moment. I wanted him. I wanted to make love to Ian.

"What happened tonight?" Ian asked.

"Shhh, not right now." I kissed up along his jaw. Our eyes met and crackling energy passed between us. I pressed my clammy forehead to his. "Later," I said.

We kissed feverishly, but Ian was holding back. Something was wrong, but I couldn't care. I needed him. I pressed my tongue into his mouth and grabbed him through his pants. He got the message and ripped the robe from my shoulders. Ian mauled my breasts. He was never so rough, but that was how I wanted it too. His hands found my garter belt and stockings. I wanted him to know I'd worn them for him tonight.

I pulled at his clothes and he tried to help me. Our faces painfully bounced together as we tried to keep kissing. It was almost funny, but neither of us was laughing. I went to my knees and peeled off his boxer-briefs. Ian's hot cock sprang out and I grabbed it, caressing as I looked up at him. I smiled and traced the rim of the head with the tip of my tongue. It occurred to me that we rarely went down on each other anymore. Ian had the strangest look on his face. What was he thinking?

Ian pulled me to my feet before I could take him in my mouth and pushed me back onto the couch. He pushed my legs back and ripped my thong away in a fury. That hurt, but it seemed appropriate. Ian had become an animal and I was his helpless prey. It was what Ray wanted to do to me. He would have taken me just like this.

"Uhhh…yesss…" I cried out when he filled me with his hardness. I was pinned to the couch.

"Are you going to tell me about tonight?" Ian groaned, his eyes wide and feral.

"I...I...thought you were watching...set me up..." I moaned, feeling his shaft move in me.

"Watching what?" He thrust hard, shifting my body.

"I...I didn't mean..." God, he felt good. This was what I needed so badly. Being made to tell him scared me and that made me burn like a supernova.

"Didn't mean what?" Another powerful thrust. He wouldn't give me what I wanted until I confessed.

"I...I kissed him...uhhhh...Ray was there...I didn't know... thought you were there...watching...uhhnnn..."

Ian was moving now. He slowly took me, drawing the truth out of me, grunting with my every word.

"I...I saw...some bad disguise...I thought...ohhh Ian...I thought you wanted..."

"Wanted what?" His voice quivered, like he was on the verge of a breakdown, but he was as hard as ever.

"Wanted to see me kiss Ray!" I cried. It was my first climax, a small one, but it was building to something more.

It looked like he wanted to say something and changed his mind. "You liked it, didn't you? An accusation. He slammed me so hard the couch shifted on the floor.

"Ian..." I couldn't speak. I couldn't tell him. Tears welled in my eyes.

"Whether I was there or not, you wanted it. You wanted him to kiss you, just like in his car."

"Ian..."

"Tell me! Tell me you liked it!" Moving faster now, demanding. Ian wanted everything. My body, my soul, my confession. "When he was behind you, touching you. When he brushed your check and kissed you..."

Wait?!? How did he know about Ray was behind me? He *was* there! He was playing with me! How dare he! I blinked away my tears and thrust back at him, driving onto his rigid staff. I was going to use him to get what I needed!

"Uhhnnn...yes! Yes, baby! I liked it when Ray kissed me! I loved it when he touched me! I wanted him!" I screamed.

"Emmm..." Ian cried.

He erupted mightily inside me and I came so hard I was dizzy. For the briefest moment I wasn't sure where I was, or even who was on top of me. In that moment, it was Ray making me cum. But then I was back and clinging to my husband. I loved him, but I was angry.

"So you *were* there?" I asked, when I caught my breath.

"I was, but I got called away by a real work emergency." I was still pinned under, his cock now limp inside me. He wouldn't look me in the eye. "How long did you stay?"

"You're such an asshole. How could you set me up like that?"

"I'm sorry. I don't know why I did it. I just wanted to see..."

"Wanted to see what?"

"I don't know exactly. I just wanted to see you..."

"Wanted to see me flirt with other men. That's what really turns you on, isn't it?"

"Yes," he said quietly, shamed. I suddenly felt guilty. I was as excited by the game as he was, but I wasn't ready to let him off the hook yet.

"Is that all you wanted to see?"

"I don't know, Emily. I swear, I don't know." He was getting very upset.

"Honey, shhh, it's okay. I'm mad you set me up, but I did have a good time. I just wish you'd come to me."

"You would have said yes?" Ian sounded shocked.

"To flirting? Probably. If Ray wasn't there, I don't know what I would have done. Christ, I can't believe I did that with a co-worker." We were still locked together and I buried my face against him, desperately hoping Ian wouldn't ask what "that" meant.

"But you did do it. You kissed him and you liked it, and it wasn't just because I was watching, was it?"

I didn't want to break his heart, but I owed him the truth. "Yes, I liked it, but I wouldn't have done it if you weren't there." That didn't explain why I let Ray touch my leg on the drive home, or why I let him grope me in the car. Ian was not there then. I said, "I liked knowing you were watching. It made me hot to know you were seeing me like that." It was the truth.

"So how long did you stay? What happened after I left?" Ian looked like he was bracing for a blow.

"When I saw you weren't there I panicked. I thought I'd done something horribly wrong, so I got out of the bar."

"That's when you called me?"

"Yes. I almost passed out when you answered the phone. You were my safety net while I was at the bar. I thought you wanted to play a game, and it was so exciting."

"But then you thought I was never there?"

"And that's why you're an asshole. I went through hell."

"But you enjoyed it?"

I couldn't look him in the eye. "God, Ian!" I tried to push him off me, but he held me on the couch.

"I enjoyed it too. It was the hottest thing I've ever seen," his voice was low, intimate.

"I know you did." I felt his cock stirring against my thigh. "But

I don't understand why."

"I can't really explain it. I like seeing you enjoy yourself…"

"Enjoy myself?" His dodge angered me.

"Okay, not just enjoy yourself. I like seeing you sexy. I like seeing other men want you."

"And if they kiss me? If they touch me?"

"I don't know. That turns me on too, crazy as it is. None of this makes sense. I know I'm nuts."

"It's a little crazy," I agreed.

"I mean, tonight was really harmless, wasn't it? It was just a kiss…" Ian left a dangling question, but I wasn't going to answer unless he asked me directly.

"It's dangerous. It could get out of hand, Ian. What if he didn't want just a kiss? What if he took me back to my car?"

I pushed Ian off of me and straddled him. His cock had throbbed back to life and I rubbed it against my swollen, slippery lips. He liked this "what if" game. I did too. I could test him. And I could relive what Ray did…

"What if it was more than kissing? Are you okay with that too?" His cock throbbed in answer. "What if I let him touch me?"

"You wouldn't…"

"I think you would like it. I think you want to see it," I taunted. God, I wanted to put him inside me.

"That thing doesn't speak for me," Ian moaned, licking his lips.

"It really turns you on, doesn't it? Thinking about Ray groping me in a dark car, sliding his hand under my dress?" We were both staring down at his cock, pointing right at me as I stroked him.

I slithered out of his lap and went on my hands and knees on the floor in front of him. I heard Ian gasp.

"He loved my garter belt. He was playing with it all night," I teased. Ian was holding back, waiting to hear more, but I had told him the truth, whether he knew it or not. It was time to push him. I reached back and I was so wet I could hear it as I rubbed myself.

"Ray pulled on my garters…uhhnnn…he pulled them while he fucked me…"

Ian pounced like a lion. He took me from behind and he fucked me feverishly. His fingers dug into the soft, white flesh of my round ass and he pulled me back into him, his guttural grunts more animal than human.

"Uhnnn…uhhnnn…ohhhh… …Fuck me! Fuck me, baby!" I cried, using language as dirty as I felt.

"Oh Emily!"

"Fuck me! Fuck me!" I was so confused. Was I begging my husband to fuck me, or was it Ray, my dream lover? It didn't matter because I came just as hard as before and slumped forward. Ian was still hard, and he still took me. Just like Ray would, I imagined. Finally, he just pulled out of me without cumming. I rolled onto my back and looked up at him, confused. I could see the anguish all over his face.

"It didn't happen. Ray didn't fuck me." I stayed close to the truth.

Ian was on top of me again, inside me again. "Did you want it to?"

He was driving me insane. What did he want to hear? The truth? A dirty lie? I went with honesty. "Maybe. I don't know."

"Really?" He sounded as confused as I was, but he was moving faster inside me now.

"I just don't know. It was so hot, kissing him with you watching, but I don't know if I could."

"Getting swept away by some handsome stranger turns you on, doesn't it?"

"Yes, baby, it does. Oh, Ian, do it. Do it, honey…"

Ian was really moving now. I wasn't going to climax again, but I wanted him to. I wanted to please him.

"Do you want to see him again?"

"Do you want me to?" I gasped, holding him to me. His hips were churning and I grabbed his butt, pulling him into me.

"Yes. I'm sorry, but I do," he confessed.

"Don't be sorry, I want to play too. I want you to see me with Ray." I couldn't believe the words were out of my mouth, but it was true! I wanted Ian to watch me with Ray.

"Ahhh…do it! Do it, Emily!" Ian cried and I felt him explode inside me.

As his weight settled onto me, I wondered, did my husband just tell me to fuck another man? I didn't know what to think. We had a *lot* to talk about.

THREE

THE NEXT MORNING my body ordered me to stay in bed, but my mind wouldn't let me be idle. Too much wine, too much sex and too much weirdness left me feeling like my skull hollowed by a melon baller. I awoke alone, with a warm dent in the bed beside me where Ian had been. The bedside clock told me we still had a couple hours before we had to get the kids and I knew we had to use that time to talk. I hoped my husband was downstairs brewing a pot of strong, black coffee.

A hot shower made me feel human again. I turned the head to a pounding massage setting and let it beat my body until the hot water finally ran out, while I tried to put all the thoughts buzzing through my brain into some kind of order. With my wet, chestnut hair pulled back into a ponytail and dressed in a tank top and boy shorts I went downstairs to find Ian did indeed put on a pot of coffee. He was sitting on the back deck, staring into the woods that bordered the rear of our yard.

"Ian, honey, why didn't you wake me?" I asked, putting a hand on his shoulder, and then bending to kiss him. I took the chair beside his.

"You looked like you needed the rest."

"That's true enough. Last night was…something."

"It was." Ian continued staring into the woods. His hand was tense around his coffee mug, like he was trying to crush it.

"You know we need to talk about last night."

"I know."

"And it can't wait. Can you look at me, Ian?" Fear seized my heart. I worried that in the cold light of day, he couldn't stand that I'd been with another man, even if it was partially his fault. I couldn't blame him, though. He may have put me in the position, but he didn't force me to do anything. That was all on me.

Finally, he turned to me, but I didn't know what to make of what I saw on that face I knew so well. I did not see anger, but grief and fear, and something else. I'd never seen that in his eyes before. It was something like lust, but darker.

"Honey," he began, and then his words came out in a torrent. "I'm so sorry. I don't know what I was thinking setting you up like that. I just thought it might be fun to play that way, because, you know, of the way we felt at Bobby's wedding."

"Ian, babe, it's okay, calm down." I took his hand and squeezed it tightly. "I don't know that it was a bad idea, I just wish you'd told me that's what you wanted to do."

He looked down. "Would you have done it?"

"I think so." My real answer was yes, but I couldn't admit that. How do you tell your husband that going out and flirting with other men in front of him turns you on?

"I wasn't sure. I knew you would like it, but I didn't know if you would do it, so I thought if I just put you there…"

"That was a shitty thing to do, Ian. And it wouldn't have worked. If I hadn't spotted you there I would have left."

"But you didn't leave." There was that gleam in his eyes again.

"No, I didn't."

"And you went over to see Ray." Was I being paranoid, or was there something strange about the way he said *Ray*?

"Yes, I wanted to teach you a lesson and since I knew it turned you on when he made a pass at me the other night, I thought it would be perfect.".

Then I quickly added, "But if I hadn't had a couple glasses of wine, and I wasn't good and pissed off, I would have never used someone I work with like that."

I did not want to think about Ray. Kissing in his car had been one thing, but we went way beyond that last night. How in the world was I ever going to face him now? I could hardly claim he'd misread my signals like the first time. And how was I going to look at him without thinking about those lips, and his hands all over me? It was my turn to look away, because I didn't want my husband to see the emotions washing across my face.

"But you did go to Ray, and I'm glad. It was hotter that it was someone you knew," Ian said, a smile playing on his lips. The dark, lusty look in his eyes was stronger.

"So you thought it was hot when I went over to see Ray? And was it hot when he kissed me?" I asked in a low voice, unsure what I wanted to hear.

"I can't lie, it was. Do you hate me?" It sounded like he hated himself enough for both of us, but I could never hate him, and I told him so.

"Of course not. I love you, Ian. I love you as much as I ever did. What happened last night wasn't…normal, but that's between us. We can do anything we like. We're two adults and whatever we choose to do in our marriage is for us to decide."

My speech seemed to take some of the burden from him, and he visibly relaxed and squeezed his hand.

"Did you like kissing Ray?" Ian asked, noticeably trying to hide is excitement.

"I'm going to be honest with you, Ian. I always will be, so don't ask me anything you really don't want the answer to."

"Okay."

"Yes, I enjoyed kissing Ray. He's handsome and I know he wants me, and that makes me feel sexy."

"How long have you known he wanted you?"

"I never thought about it before this week. We've always flirted, but I never thought it meant anything. He knows I'm married."

"Guys don't care about that so much, Emily. If they want to fuck you and you give them an opening they'll go for it."

I laughed. He was probably right, but we women never like to admit that. "It's like that *When Harry Met Sally* thing. I guess men and women can't really be friends if there's an attraction. But I don't know if Ray wants to…fuck…me." It was hard to spit the word out. Just saying it made me think of doing it, and that led my mind to places it probably shouldn't go.

"He does. Trust me," Ian replied knowingly.

"How could you possibly know that?"

"I, uh, just know the type and I saw how he was looking at you. He wanted you."

"And that turns you on?" I just didn't understand that. Husbands are supposed to be jealous and protective, right?

"It does. Seeing how other guys want you really turns me on. Watching you flirting with Ray in that sexy dress last night was incredible, Emily. It was like I was seeing you for the first time."

"And you weren't jealous at all?"

"I guess a tiny bit, but no, not really. I was too into it to be turned on. And it was hot because I knew you liked it too."

I couldn't help blushing. "I feel like I got the better end of the deal, though. I got to have all the fun. I don't think I could handle watching you with another woman."

"I don't want another woman. I only want you, Emily. It's always been you."

"And I just want you…" The sentence dangled from my lips, because it wasn't the whole truth. I was perfectly happy with Ian and had no desire to go out and sleep with other men. I would never go looking for it, but when it just happened to me, I couldn't help but enjoy it.

"But?"

"There's no 'but,' really. It's just that yes, an attractive younger guy coming onto makes me feel sexy and with you there, looking on, I felt like I had permission to maybe play a little bit. But that doesn't mean I'm not happy with you."

"I know."

"And I could never do that without you there. You're my safety net. I know things won't go too far if you're there. I mean, it was hotter *because* you were there. I don't want us to turn into one of those couples where we're just the mom and the dad and you don't see me as a woman anymore. It was like, I could show you how sexy I am—and even show you I can still be dirty and hot. And since I know it turns you on, that just makes it so much better." I had to stop because I was getting myself aroused just talking about it. I saw the tent in Ian's shorts. He liked it just as much as I did. But we needed to have a serious talk. We couldn't let ourselves get sidetracked.

"Did you stop when you realized I wasn't there?" Ian's voice was husky.

I looked away. "Not right away. I mean, I knew I should, but Ray was insistent. When I went outside, he went with me. Ray was there when we spoke on the phone then he drove me out to my car."

"Did he kiss you goodnight?"

"Yes. I mean, after everything else, that didn't seem so bad." I bit my lip. That just slipped out.

"What was 'everything else?'" Ian looked at me like a deer in headlights.

"I didn't have sex with him, you have to know that, okay? Do you really want to know everything?"

I watched him war with himself as he decided. Finally, he said, "No, not this time."

"This time?" I was shocked.

"How did you leave things with Ray?" Ian ignored my question.

"I got out of the car and came home. We didn't really talk. What did you mean *this time*?"

"I...I think we should play again. I think you should hook up with Ray."

"What? Ian, I have to work with him! I don't want to be the office slut! You're crazy!"

"Listen, hear me out. I like that it's Ray *because* you work with him. It makes it more dangerous, and that makes it more exciting."

"Right, but you don't have to deal with the fallout. I do." Now I thought he'd lost his mind. I could not go out and hook up with Ray again. I wasn't adverse to playing, but just not with Ray.

"Didn't you mention he's leaving soon?"

"Yeah, they've transferred him to the office in Philadelphia. He's only got two more weeks here, but that's not that point. You're right, it is dangerous."

"But because he's leaving it's not *so* dangerous. Think about it, Emily. It could just be a little goodbye fling, then he's gone and it's over. Once he leaves, there's nothing to worry about." Ian was trying very hard to convince me.

"Philly's only a couple hours by train," I teased, but that didn't take the wind out of his sails.

"You really want this, don't you?" I asked.

"I do. Come on, Emily. Last night was amazing. I know you felt it too. Where's the harm in playing around for a couple weeks if it's going to make us feel like that?"

I could have given him a hundred reasons. Any sane person could have, but maybe I'm crazy too, because I didn't give him one. I really wanted to play, too.

"Why does it have to be Ray?" I asked

"I told you. I know you like him. I saw how much you liked teasing him, but this time it won't just be a tease."

"You just want me to ask him on a date?" I couldn't believe I was on the verge of agreeing to this.

"Just let him know you had a good time last night. Trust me, he'll do the rest."

"So then, I go out with him and what happens? You know you have to be there, right? I want you watching me."

"I guess you guys go out and see what happens, that's all. I know it will be great."

"And if something does happen? How much should happen, Ian? What if he tries to get me alone?"

"Go out to his car or something. I can sneak up and keep an eye on you," he replied eagerly.

"You didn't answer me. How far should I go?" I asked carefully.

"Just go with it. Do whatever feels natural."

"Ian…"

"I trust you, okay? We're in this together. Do you have Ray's number?"

"It's in my phone."

"Go get it."

I wasn't sure what he was up to. When I went into the house to get my cell phone, I thought about what he'd said. *Do whatever feels natural?* Was there anything natural about this? I knew from last night that it would be very easy to get carried away with Ray. I was confident I wouldn't have sex with him, especially not in his car, but where would I stop? Could Ian really handle it if he saw Ray touching me like he did last night? God, just thinking about it, I could feel Ray's brief touch on my pussy. My bizarre conversation with my husband this morning had me almost as horny as the night before – so much that I and wondered if we had time for a quickie before we had to get the kids.

Ian took the phone from me and found Ray's number. He started typing.

"What did you do?" I snatched my phone back, but it was too late. Ian had texted Ray: *Great time last night. Can't wait to see you Monday.*

"Ian!" I shrieked.

He cut off my protest with a kiss and I melted into it. Ian wasn't going to need much coaxing to get me out of my clothes. Luckily, we have a high privacy fence on either side of our backyard. The only way a neighbor could see was if they really made an effort. Thinking about that possibility turned me on even more. Ian pulled at my tank top and drew it over my head. The morning air crinkled my long nipples to hardness and he lightly teased them with his fingers.

"Ian…"

"We're going to play, aren't we?" He kissed my neck, melting my resistance.

"Yesss…" I didn't care if it was a bad idea. It was too hot to resist. I could be a vixen for the next two weeks, then go back to my normal life. What woman wouldn't want that?

My phone chirped and Ian grabbed it, turning his back to me. He chuckled and said, "Ray says he can't stop thinking about last night. Says you can talk at the gym. Hey, you never mentioned you work out with him."

"I don't," I said, trying to get the phone back. God knew what else Ian would send out. "He goes to my gym, but we don't work out together. Gimme that!"

Ian typed out another message and then turned and pushed me back on the lounge. My eyes widened when he snapped a picture with the phone, holding it at an angle where I would look like I took the picture. I tried to chase him across the deck, but he sent the message anyway.

"I can't believe you just sent him a topless picture of me!" I got the phone back. Ian had texted: *here's something to really think about!*

"You are out of your mind!" I protested.

"And you love every second of it."

Ian turned me and bent me forward over the deck railing. He pulled down my boy shorts and there was a rustling as he dropped his shorts. In a moment, he was inside me and I moaned deeply. I gripped the railing and he held my shoulders as he took me.

"Admit it, you like Ray having that picture." Ian grunted.

"Ian...I...yesss..." I thought about Ray getting hard after seeing me topless and it sent a thrill to my toes.

"You can't wait to go out with him again..."

"Yesss...Ian...fuck me! I can't wait to kiss him while you watch us, baby!"

"Uhhnnn..."

"He's gonna kiss meee...and touch meee...and...ohhhh...I'm gonna touch him..."

"Touch his dick…"

"Yess…"

"Suck it…"

"Yesss…oh yessss…babyyy… You like that? You want me see me suck his cock?"

"Uhhnnn…yessss…"

Neither of us could speak after that. Ian took my bouncing breasts in his hands and pinched and pulled my nipples and I came hard, the orgasm taking my strength so that I sagged against the railing. Ian kept going right through my climax and soon, he was cumming too, filling me while he drove up inside me. He pressed into my back and the hard wood of the railing dug into me, but it didn't matter.

"I love you, honey. I love you so much."

"I love you too, Emily."

FOUR

To CALL THE rest of the weekend "loving" would be a gross under-statement. Ian and I couldn't keep our hands off each other and we really had to make an effort to cool it when the kids were around. But once we put them to sleep, we were all over each other, sharing fantasy details of my future date with Ray. The more we role-played, the more excited I became about the idea. I worried I was going to melt into a puddle when I saw Ray on Monday. His only response to my picture had been: *WOW!* Ian and I decided to leave it there.

Monday morning was hectic as usual. Once the nanny arrived and took over, Ian came up to the bedroom and hung around, which was odd. Usually, he gets ready for work and spends time in the kitch-en with the kids and chatting up the nanny, a pretty, chubby girl in her early twenties named Natalie. But this morning he sat on the bed and watched as I got ready for work. It was sexy having him watch me, and I took my time, putting special care into it. After all, I was getting ready to see my new "boyfriend," wasn't I? Ian seemed eager to see what I was wearing for Ray, although I was sure nothing would happen at work.

I chose a light gray suit with one of my shorter skirts, something I had not worn in quite some time. Working around mostly men, I have to be careful about my attire. I like looking good, but I can't be too obviously sexy or they start talking. Today, I was willing to risk showing a little more. Ian watched me closely as I walked back and forth in front of him wearing nothing but a little black thong. I added a matching bra that would really push me up and fill out my tailored jacket. Then I stood right next to Ian to put on my stockings. He eagerly watched as I placed a foot on the bed and rolled one silky stocking up my leg, then the other. Ian ran his fingers up the smooth sheath of my calf and I sighed.

"I really love you in stockings," he said.

"I know you do," I smiled.

"But you always said you hated them."

"That's because garter belts are a pain in the butt, but these stay up on their own and they make me feel sexy." I snapped the top against my thigh for emphasis and leaned over to share a soft, sensual kiss with Ian. "I know you're looking at my ass," I said as I walked back to the bathroom. I pulled on a black camisole to wear under my jacket. Only the lace trim at the top would show, and hopefully give Ray some ideas. The heels I selected were higher than I usually wear for work, but they made my legs look great.

"Let me know how lunch goes," Ian said when we kissed and parted at the front door.

It was the longest train ride of my life, taking me closer and closer to doing something I couldn't take back. Once I made it clear to Ray I was available, I knew I'd be taking a step that lead Ian and I into a new life. It wasn't permanent, but for the next two weeks I would actively be engaged in an affair with another man. Was it okay because my husband wanted me to do it? The thing that made me feel so guilty was how badly I wanted it. I wanted to be with Ray again, and I wanted Ian to see me being a dirty little -- I hate to admit it – a dirty little slut.

I was always such a good girl, so proper. I did what was expected and behaved and made sure not to cause waves. I certainly did not dress up to entice men who weren't my husband. But even on the train that morning, I knew the men noticed me. I sat with my legs crossed and my hands in my lap and pretended not to see the lustful glances that came my way. The skirt looked very short when I sat like that and I really felt like I was putting on a show for them. When we pulled into the station, I slowly uncrossed my legs before standing and put an extra wiggle into my hips as I walked onto the platform. Playing the dirty little slut was a fun game!

My antenna was up as soon as I entered the office. I figured Ray would be lurking somewhere close to my cubicle, but he wasn't anywhere to be found. I lingered in the break room when I went for coffee, but didn't see him there either. I could have gone around to his cubicle, but I didn't want to seem like I was looking for him, so I just went back to my desk and tried to work. It was difficult to focus on what I was writing. With everything going through my head, what I turned out was probably crap, but I could always go back and redo it. I just needed to keep busy or my nerves were going to get to me.

"Hey there," Ray said, silently entering my cubicle behind me. I nearly fell out of my chair and turned to face him.

"Hi, Ray. I was wondering where you were this morning." I strained to sound casual.

"I had an early meeting. I've got to start transitioning stuff off my plate before the transfer." He checked out my legs as I crossed them. "Damn, you look good this morning. Is that for me?"

I tried not to respond to that charming smile. "Why would I be dressing for you?" A smile creased my lips.

"No reason, I guess. Doesn't matter anyway. You look hot in everything."

"Thanks," I replied, blushing.

Ray looked to make sure the hallway was clear, and knelt down. He slid his hand up my smooth, nylon-covered leg. I sighed and only put my hand over his when he tried to go under my skirt.

"Ray…"

"What? I was just wondering if you were wearing stockings again. Do you mind me checking?"

I was speechless. His hand was so hot on my leg and I wanted him to touch me, but we were in the office! And Ian wasn't around. It didn't seem right to do this without my husband there.

"No, I don't mind," I whispered. "But not here. Anyone could walk by." He pressed forward and I allowed him just under the hem of my skirt, where he fingered the lacy top of my stocking.

"I thought so," he grinned. "I guess I'll see you at the gym."

He blew me a kiss and left, leaving me flushed and dry-mouthed, wondering just what I was really getting into. Ian and I wanted to play this game, but I realized Ray was a wild card. He didn't have to play by our rules. That made everything so much more dangerous. I would have to be careful to keep control.

Later, we walked to the gym together, but I couldn't bring myself to do anything but make small talk. I was waiting for Ray to make a move, but all he did was ask if we could work out together. Otherwise, he stuck to flirting, but it wasn't the same. I noticed a new edge to it. He said all the typical things, but he was looking at me differently now. His eyes seemed to linger on my body, from the curve of my butt in that skirt to the swell of my breasts in the tailored jacket. He looked at me with a new hunger, not like he was just admiring me, but like he expected to taste me. It caused tingles all over and made me hope he'd kiss me.

It was only worse once we got to the gym. I emerged from the locker room and found Ray over by the free weights, and he took it upon himself to be my personal trainer.

"You've got some body, Em," he said, nakedly appraising me. I'm not one of those women who run around the gym half-naked, but I suddenly felt very exposed in my workout gear. I had a snug pink and white racer-back Lycra tank top, with a bra built-in, but like most workout gear, it did nothing to hide my erect nipples. The black yoga pants hugged my butt like a second skin, but everyone wears those.

"It's a shame you have to hide it under suits every day," he added.

"I can't come to work naked just to make you happy." I laughed.

"How about you just come to my place that way?"

"I don't know that I could trust you if we were alone."

"I would be the perfect gentleman. I wouldn't ask you to do anything you didn't want to."

Our banter went on like that while he handed me a set of ten-pound weights and put me through some reps. It gave him an excuse to touch me, as he guided my arms and made sure I kept the correct form. It was only casual touching, but given my dirty thoughts, it was hardly casual for me. The excitement I felt the other night picked up right where it left off, and I realized this game Ian wanted to play was going to be more fun than I thought. When I finished, Ray did his reps and it was quite a sight to see his arms flex as he lifted those heavy dumbbells. His t-shirt had the sleeves cut off, so I didn't miss a muscle. I just wished he had no shirt at all. And his little shorts really showed off his butt, too. I'd seen him do squats before, and they really paid off. I did my butt work on the Stairmaster.

When I moved on to the butterfly machine, Ray didn't even try to pretend he wasn't staring at my breasts as I raised my arms to the side. In my mind, he just stepped forward and grabbed them, teasing my nipples until I fell to my knees in front of him. The half-hour at the gym left me soaking wet, and not just drenched in sweat.

Ray waited for me outside and we walked back to the office. He asked me to stop with him in the adjoining parking garage so he could drop his gym bag in his car. I agreed, both excited and scared that we were going to be someplace more secluded. I tried keeping my distance while Ray popped his trunk and put his bag in it, but as soon as he closed the lid, he pulled me into his arms.

"Someone might see us," I complained, but it was a bluff. The dimly-lit, cool concrete parking garage was empty, except for us. I heard the opening and closing of doors, and tires squealing in the distance, but our level was clear.

"There's no one here," he replied, and moved in for a kiss.

His lips were firm and insistent, and I just melted under his advance. I could never tire of his kisses. He maneuvered me back a couple steps and I was pressed against a cool, concrete pillar beside his car. I held his face and then felt his rock-hard shoulders, while his hands went from my narrow waist to my butt. He massaged my cheeks, bringing my already short skirt higher. I avidly sucked his tongue into my mouth and moaned when he moved to kissing the side of my neck. When he kneaded my breast, it felt great—even through my jacket. He started to unbutton it, and that's when I finally stopped him.

"Ray, we're going to be late. We've got to get back to the office," I whimpered, weakly pushing him away.

"You can't keep leaving me like this, Em. I want you so damn bad," he panted.

"I know. I know."

"Let's go out after work. We'll go somewhere quiet."

"But there's my husband, and my kids. I can't just disappear," I protested. "Tomorrow. I'll tell Ian I'm going out with my girlfriend Christine for dinner. We can hang out for a couple hours. Okay?"

"Alright. Tomorrow night then. How about I cook for you?"

I knew why Ray wanted me alone, but that couldn't happen. We had to be out in public, so Ian could be there. I was supposed to "date" Ray, not just go back to his place and screw him. I felt guilty enough for making out with Ray just now. Ian and I had left things kind of open, with his *just do what feels natural* pronouncement, but I didn't feel comfortable fooling around without Ian with me, even if I suspected he'd encourage me to do it. Wasn't it just cheating then? There was nothing *natural* about any of this.

"Let's meet at Bar 88 again. I've never done anything like this. I can't just go to your place. I hope you understand, Ray."

"I do, Em. It's okay. We'll hang out and have a good time. It's cool."

We kissed again and went back to work. I stopped at the ladies' room, splashed some cold water on my face, then, as soon as I got back to my desk, I texted Ian:

-Worked out with Ray. Date night tomorrow night. He kissed me.

I waited nervously for Ian's reply, afraid he'd be angry that I let Ray kiss me without him being there. I needn't have worried.

Ian replied:

-Excellent. Details tonight. Can't wait.

I sighed. I wanted this too, but I just couldn't help worrying that we were in too deep already.

***

"What are you going to wear tonight?" Ian eagerly asked when I walked into our bedroom in my little red, silk kimono, fresh from the shower. He'd been like since I got home from work yesterday, following me around like a puppy dog and peppering me with questions about my "date." I had questions myself, but as before, Ian doggedly refused to answer them. He just would not tell me what he thought should happen between me and Ray. I could have stood my ground and insisted he give me clear boundaries, but honestly, I didn't want to know what he would say. And maybe—deep down—I didn't want any boundaries.

"I've got something in mind that I think Ray will like, but nothing like the other night. I was way overdressed for that place."

"You looked hot."

"Thanks, but I thought tonight I would go more casual." I went to my lingerie drawer and selected an ivory lace-trimmed bra with a small bow in the center and the matching panties. I laid them on the bed and saw Ian was following my every move. "Are you going to watch me get ready?"

"I think it's sexy."

I pushed between his legs and put my arms over his shoulders, so my chest, barely covered by the kimono, was right in his face. When I stroked his hair, he looked up at me. "It's turning you on to watch me get ready for a date with another man, isn't it?"

"Is that a problem?" he asked. His thumbs easily stroked my nipples to hardness through the thin silk of my robe. I smiled and kissed him. He opened the flimsy knot in my belt and parted the robe. His smooth hands covered my breasts, lightly pulling my long hard nipples. I pulled away from the kiss and sighed.

"If you keep doing that, I'll never get out of here," I moaned, trying to push away from him. But he cupped my mound and squeezed firmly, I leaned into him as warm pleasure flooded my body. It was crazy, but I thought maybe he wanted me horny before going out with Ray. Maybe he thought more would happen if I was already in the mood before I left. Either that, or he wanted to have sex before I left, but oddly, I was not comfortable with that. I didn't want to meet Ray fresh from another man's bed, even if that other man was my husband.

"Okay, I'll let you get ready then," he replied, releasing me after a final lick of my nipple. I guess he wouldn't let anything get in the way of my date.

After I dressed in my panties and bra—which gave my breasts a little boosted—I returned to the bathroom to blow out my hair and do my make-up. I normally go with a more natural look, but as with the night we played the game, I went with more kohl around my eyes and a deep red lipstick. Looking in the mirror, I thought it showed I meant business. I wore my hair loose and just ran a brush through it.

Ian was still on the bed when I came back out and he watched me finish dressing. Knowing I wouldn't have to worry about being chilly on that warm summer night, I dug an old denim skirt from the back of the closet. I'd only ever worn it once because it was just too damned short. I spent that whole night pulling it down because I couldn't help feeling like my ass was hanging out. Slipping into it, the skirt still seemed too short, but that was a plus where Ray was concerned. I'd just have to walk with confidence to pull it off. I paired the skirt with a snug, deep purple cardigan that I usually wore with a tank top underneath because of its low neckline, but tonight I wanted to show off some skin. The only thing I added was a heart-shaped pendant that drew the eye down toward my cleavage.

When I finished, I posed for Ian, who gave me his enthusiastic approval. "Ray is going to love you tonight. You look hot, but sweet," my husband told me. He wanted a kiss, but I avoided it. I didn't want my lipstick smeared before my date.

***

Bar88 was even more crowded than before, but I had no trouble finding Ray. He had the same pool table in the corner staked out and was working it by himself. I wondered how long he'd been there. He looked good in a nice, gray untucked dress shirt and jeans. Casual, but put together. He seemed in perfect control of his body as he worked his way around the table to make his shots. He leaned forward and the shirt pulled tight across his shoulders, reminding me how built he was underneath it.

I was so nervous and excited as I watched Ray. We were really doing this! I was going on a date with another man while my husband hid and watched it unfold. I couldn't help thinking Ian and I were insane, or perverted at the very least. So many questions and conflicting feelings had been going through my mind ever since I agreed to this. Sure, I told myself I was doing this for Ian, but that wasn't entirely true. I liked it when Ray kissed me, and the thought of him doing it again gave me the chills. I still wasn't sure I could go all the way and have sex with him, but a little fooling around like before would be okay.

Then again, how could I think that was okay? Was it just because my husband not only approved, but encouraged it? And was that reason enough? I'll admit, knowing that it made Ian horny to watch me misbehave really, really turned me on. I could be as bad as I wanted to be and still go home to my family and our picture-perfect suburban life. It was a dream come true.

I watched Ray until I saw Ian enter the bar and head up into the balcony. He'd followed me in his car, but didn't want to walk in with me. Once Ian was safely ensconced upstairs, I walked up behind Ray and ran my hand over his back. He looked up with a smile, then pulled me close with an arm around my waist and we kissed. I closed my eyes and only barely resisted accepting his tongue. Ian and I never kissed like that in public, but I couldn't help myself with Ray.

"Hey, beautiful. You look hot," he said, looking down at my outfit. I liked that he didn't even pretend he was doing anything other than trying to bed me.

"Thanks. I hope I didn't keep you waiting long."

"I always expect women to be late. I ordered you a glass of wine."

"That was thoughtful," I replied, taking the glass from the small, round table by the wall and sipping from it. "Unless you're just trying to get me drunk."

"I don't think I need to get you drunk."

"Oh no?"

"Nope. I think you can be bad all on your own."

"I don't know about that. We'll have to see, I guess."

Ray backed me against the table and we kissed again. This time, his hand went to my firm ass, which he gave a good, hard squeeze. It was funny how things I would never be comfortable with doing before were okay, even desirable, with Ray. I would never let my husband just paw me like that in public.

"You'd better behave yourself, Ray. We can't do it right here." I giggled.

"We can always go somewhere else, like my place."

"Why don't you rack the balls instead and we'll play a game?"

"Strip pool?" Ray suggested as he went around for the rack.

"Um, I'm not taking my clothes off here."

"The stripping would come later."

I bent over the table as I rolled the eight ball to him and like a magnet my low-cut sweater drew his eyes. I wondered if he could make out the cute little bow between my breasts. When the table was ready he asked if I wanted to break, then he stood behind me while I bent over to take the shot. The little denim skirt rode up, and I knew he was looking at my ass. I just might have bent farther forward than I had to, but I dare anyone to prove it. I was solids right away I sank the ball in the side pocket with a solid straight shot, and brushed against Ray as I went around to line up the next.

But it was hard to play with Ray watching me because I was putting just as much effort into posing for him as I was into playing. The first game went swiftly and he won easily. He went to the bar for another round while I set up for the next game.

Ian was in the same seat, watching us from the balcony. I flashed him a smile while Ray was gone, but I couldn't read his face from so far away. What was he thinking while he watched me flirt with Ray? Did Ian get hard when Ray grabbed my ass, or was he pissed that I gave my date liberties I never gave him? I still had the feeling this could all go horribly wrong, but I didn't want to stop playing.

Ray returned quickly and, along with the fresh drink—he'd replaced my glass of cabernet with a sangria—he had two tequila shots. I just looked at him with my hands on my hips, tapping a foot in its wedge-heeled sandal.

"I thought you weren't trying to get me drunk," I said.

"I'm not. I just assumed you could handle a shot." His innocent act was not very convincing.

"Mixing wine and tequila is not a good idea. Besides, what do you think I am, some silly little co-ed? I don't do shots anymore."

"Sorry, I just thought you wanted to have fun tonight. Isn't this about breaking out? You could have chosen to stay home in your cozy little house and make a casserole and watch cartoons with your husband and the kids, but you didn't. You wanted to come out with me, so come on and live a little." He held up one of the shots.

"You're good," I said. I knew full-well he was trying to manipulate me, and I was letting him. I took the shot and he shook some salt onto his wrist. I gave him a wry smile and used plenty of tongue when I sucked the salt from him. I knocked back the shot and he held up the lime wedge. I sucked his fingertips when I took the fruit. "You're turn," I said, when I was finished.

Feeling saucy, I swept my hair to the side, licked my fingers, and swiped my skin to create a wet a spot on my neck. I turned to make sure I could see Ian while Ray went for it. My husband was practically leaning over the railing and very obviously staring, like he didn't care if he got caught. I hoped Ray didn't notice some guy staring at us. I dabbed the wet spot with salt and Ray moved right in, heartily sucking on my neck before downing his shot, giving me the chills. I smiled for Ian, and then pulled Ray in for a kiss after he sucked his lime. The citrusy taste was nice. This time, I slipped Ray my tongue, eyes open through the whole kiss so I could watch Ian. I could feel my pussy tighten with need as I watched Ian watching us.

"How about playing for stakes this time?" Ray asked, while I caught my breath.

"It depends. What do you have in mind?"

"First up, if I can sink two balls of the same color on the break, you have to undo a button on your sweater."

"Ray..." I protested. The sweater was low-cut as it was. If I opened a button, neither Ray nor anyone else would have to try very hard to look into my sweater. But wasn't he right? Wasn't I there to break out of my everyday life and play at being someone else? Besides, I'd seen him play and I knew he only had a fifty-fifty shot of making it happen. I fixed his eyes, smiled slyly and said, "Alright. But if you miss, you have to do another shot, and I don't."

"You've got a deal," he replied confidently.

I stood to the side, and of course Ray made the shot, but then he was motivated, wasn't he? He was triumphant as he walked over to me and waited. I moved, to make sure he wasn't blocking Ian's view, and popped open the top button on my sweater. The tequila was already having an effect on me, and I tugged at the hem of my clingy sweater so that the button fell open and the lacy edge of my bra peaked out. I tried as hard as I could to control myself, but I'm sure I blushed just a little bit anyway.

"Now that's more like it," Ray grinned.

"And that's all I'm doing in here," I warned.

"Okay. How about you owe me a kiss for every ball I sink, and if I win the game you have to go wherever I want afterward?"

He certainly was bound and determined to get me into bed.

"I'm not going back to your place, Ray," I answered.

"Not my place, no."

"And not a hotel," I added, thinking on my feet.

"Not a hotel, either," he agreed.

"Okay." Goosebumps crawled all across my skin as I wondered what I was getting into. Ray wanted to screw me, so where would be take me to try and accomplish that? What if he took me somewhere Ian couldn't follow? I realized that Ian and I hadn't really thought everything through. We should have assumed Ray would try to get me alone at some point. I was sure Ian would want me to go, as long as he could be there to see what happened. The danger turned me on, but I also worried about the consequences.

"And what about when you make your shots or win?" he asked me.

I took a long drink of liquid courage. "The kissing part sounds about right, but you've got to kiss how I want you to…"

"Okay, that sounds interesting."

"…And if I win, then I get to decide where we go." I had no idea where I could take Ray, but I would think of something. Maybe we could just fool around in his car and Ian could sneak close enough to see us.

"Alright, then. Let's do this."

The stakes were high, so I put actual effort into playing. Ian had taught me years ago when we were dating. I got pretty good when we played on a regular basis, but that was years ago. I found I still had some skills, but my head was swimming from the tequila and I was still distracted by the way Ray checked me out when I bent over the table. I felt like my breasts were going to spill out of my bra when I leaned forward. I would have worn something different if I knew half the bar was going to see it.

And Ray was not the only one looking. The guys at the surrounding tables, either behind me or in front, seemed to pause their games when I took a shot. All that attention was having quite an effect on me, and I felt my panties get damp. Things only got worse when halfway through the game, Ray decided to start collecting his kisses early.

"Why wait?" he asked, pulling me to him. It was a hot, quick kiss, but then there was another, and another, and the kisses were lasting longer and getting hotter. I went for it when he gave me his tongue and let him grope me as much as he wanted, knowing full well we were putting on a show for the guys around us. But the real show was for Ian. I kept glancing up at him, wishing I knew what he was thinking. Toward the end of the game, I realized he'd disappeared from his perch, and I wondered if it was too much for him.

"Looks like I win!" Ray announced after sinking the eight ball. He'd been taunting me for a while, but I was so horny I didn't care. Dangerous as it was, I know part of me wanted him to win. I didn't care where he took me, and that was crazy. He pulled me in for one last, long victory kiss and he said he was going to go pay our tab.

I went to the bathroom to freshen up and nearly walked right into Ian when I turned the corner to go down the long corridor. He had the oddest look on his face. It was just like the night Ray dropped me off at home. He looked pained, but I also knew he wanted to pull me into the bathroom and fuck me on the spot. Honestly, I don't know if I would have stopped him.

"Honey, I don't have much time. Ray wants to take me someplace, but I don't know where," I whispered hurriedly.

"Do it," he said and pulled me into a kiss. Having two men who couldn't get enough of me was a heady feeling, but I had to push my husband away. I had to get back before Ray came looking for me, and I really did need to use the ladies' room. He looked hurt that I pushed him away.

"Are you sure? I could just tell him I have to get home."

"Do it, Em. I'll follow you guys. Just try to make sure I can see you guys." His eyes were on fire.

"What if he wants to…"

"I trust you. Just do what comes naturally."

There was that phase again, as if any of this was natural. If Ian wanted me to go for it, I would. I was just afraid my resistance would falter once I was in Ray's arms again. I repeated in my head: *You will not sleep with him. You will not sleep with him.* I gave Ian another peck and disappeared into the ladies room. I took care of business then touched up my hair and make-up. I really was hanging out of that sweater! No wonder all those guys couldn't keep their eyes off of me! I repositioned my breasts in the bra, and just barely resisted redoing that top button.

Ian was waiting outside the bathroom and with a kiss, he wished me luck.

My other man, Ray, waited by the bar and told me he would

meet me by the door after he used the bathroom. I thought about how funny it would be if Ray and Ian ran into each other. Would Ian be able to play it cool? With as horny as he's been since we started our game, I could picture him slapping Ray on the back and telling him to have fun!

What had I gotten myself into?

I waited outside, thankful for the slight breeze, and tried not to think about all the ways this could get out of hand. Ray was gone longer than I thought he'd be, but he looked very happy when he came outside. He took my hand and led me to the Mercedes.

"I'll bring you back for your car," he said.

"I can't stay out too late. I have to get home at some point or my husband is going to wonder what I'm up to," I warned, hoping that would slow him down.

He just smiled. "I won't keep you any longer than you want me to." He held the door, looking at my legs as my skirt rode up when I slid into the powerful, dark machine. I purposely did not fix my skirt. When Ray got into the car, I pulled him into a long kiss, hoping to give Ian long enough to get out to his car and into a position to follow us.

"So where are we going?" I asked.

"It's not too far. You'll know soon enough."

It was a short drive, but an eventful one. My sweater gaped open and Ray had one eye on my breasts the entire time. When he wasn't shifting and gunning the motor to roar away from the intersections as soon as the lights flashed green, his hand was on my leg. His fingers continually danced by my inner thigh, and I gave him plenty of leeway. His touch made my heart beat faster, but I stopped him before he could reach my panties. I didn't want him to feel that my panties were already damp. I didn't want him to think I was *too* easy. Ray didn't need to know how much willpower it took to stop him each time.

"You'd better concentrate on the road," I warned. The way he drove scared and excited me. I could feel the deep bass snarl of the engine right through my seat every time he gunned the motor. I just hoped Ian could keep up in our Camry.

We pulled into the lot of a large condo complex and at first, I thought Ray had taken me back to his place anyway. I was prepared to shut him right down. I just could not let him take me someplace that private. It would ruin my plans with Ian. He drove around to the back of the lot and parked by a line of tall shrubs. Behind them was a high, black wrought-iron fence. Ray shut off the engine and announced he'd arrived.

"Arrived where? Is this your complex?"

"It is, but before you freak out, I am not taking you up to my place, unless you really want to go."

"I don't."

"Then come with me."

Confused, but before I could protest further, Ray climbed out of the car and walked away, leaving me no choice but to follow. I heard the faint hum of a motor and the trickling of water. Through the fence, I saw a large pool in the darkness, only dimly lit by lights beneath the water. The pool was obviously closed, so it couldn't be a midnight swim he had in mind, or so I thought. When I caught up with Ray he was working the combination lock that held the gate closed.

"What are you doing? The pool is closed," I whispered.

"Not if you know the combination," he grinned.

"And how would you know that? Are you a lifeguard on the side?"

"No, but I got to know her quite well this summer."

"I bet." I could just imagine Ray working his charms on some blonde, tanned twenty-year-old co-ed. Why did that make me jealous?

"Juliet told me the security camera in the pool area doesn't actually work and gave me the combination so I could take a midnight swim if I wanted."

"Sounds like it was an invitation."

"A gentleman never tells."

Ray unsnapped the lock and pulled the chain free as quietly as possible. I was dubious, but when he held the gate open, I slipped through it. I looked over my shoulder, but couldn't see any sign of my husband in the dark parking lot. Ray followed me through and laced the chain back through the bars.

There was a large concrete apron around the pool, surrounded by white metal chaise lounges which had been stripped of their cushions for the night. At one end was a cinder block pool house with a shed beside it. A lifeguard stand towered over the deep end of the pool. It seemed that if we stayed by the deep end, the shrubs and the pool house would block anyone from the condo having a clear view. Ian would still be able to watch us if he squeezed through the shrubs and looked through the fence. When I turned, Ray was right there and he put his arms around me.

"I'm not going skinny dipping," I told him as forcefully as I could between kisses.

"That's too bad, because I'm going in. We could leave our underwear on. That's just like a bathing suit."

I hardly thought my sexy bra and panties were like the two-piece suits I usually wore to the beach. "I don't know, Ray. If we get caught, we could get in real trouble."

"If we're quiet no one will know we're here," he said. He unbuttoned his shirt.

Almost no one, I thought. I was frozen by fear and just watched as Ray shed his shirt, and then kicked off his shoes and dropped his jeans. I really wanted him to shed his black boxer briefs too, but he didn't. Instead, he blew me a kiss then eased silently into the water. He kicked off the side and glided out until he was in the middle of the pool looking up at me. He didn't speak, but his face said everything. His look was a challenge. *Well?* He seemed to ask.

My first consideration was what Ian wanted me to do. I couldn't see him, but I was sure he was there in the darkness, watching us. I wished I could see him. Without being there to back me up, my confidence faltered. I knew that Ian wanted me to strip down and join Ray in the pool. My husband probably wanted to see me nude, but I was not getting naked with Ray. I needed the protection of my clothes in case I wasn't strong enough to tell Ray no.

But it wasn't really what Ian wanted that spurred me to start me unbuttoning my sweater. No, I thought about Ray, by the pool with that young lifeguard, and how she probably shed her red swimsuit for him without a second thought. I could see that blonde showing Ray a good time and I did not want to be outdone. Ray wanted to see me and after all those months of sneaking peeks to check me out. It was time to give him what he wanted.

I waited a beat between each button, then peeled back my sweater like I was making a great reveal. Ray's huge grinned boosted my confidence. I tossed my sweater onto one of the skeletal lounges unsnapped my skirt and shimmied out of it, relieved I hadn't worn a thong, as had become my habit. My skirt joined my sweater on the lounge and I sashayed to the edge of my pool in nothing but my lacy bra, panties and high, wedge-heeled sandals. Ray swam close to the edge and looked right up at me when I stepped out of my sandals.

"Damn," he whistled. "I knew you were hot, but I had no idea."

I looked down at him between my breasts and smiled.

"Don't shout when you come in. It's a little cold," he warned.

A little cold was an understatement. I sat on the edge and almost backed out when I put my legs into the clear water. But I gritted my teeth, adjusted my position, then Ray put his hands on my sides and pulled me into the pool. The water was chilly, but he was warm and held me tight against him as he took us away from the side.

"I can swim on my own, you know," I said.

I pushed away and floated on my back. Ray held onto my feet and the cool evening air on my soaked body made my nipples achingly hard. I also realized that my soaked underwear was virtually transparent and I fought the urge to cover myself. Ray pulled me closer again, parting my legs so that he was between them. His hands slid up my legs, over my hips and tummy, and then over my breasts. I gasped when his thumbs brushed my nipples and I moved into his arms and kissed him.

"You know, if the guys at work knew I was here with you right now, half-naked, they would all be incredibly jealous," he said, massaging my butt as he held me close. I wrapped my legs around his waist and his hard-on nestled into the cleft between my legs. It was so intimate that, for a moment, I thought I must be dreaming. I wasn't really there, was I? With another man holding and kissing me? I was sure Ian was with us. I could feel him watching, and it emboldened me.

"I doubt that's true."

"Please, they all want to fuck you in the worst way." His cock pulsed against me and I knew that at least he did.

"Now I know you're lying."

"You don't expect me to believe you don't notice the guys checking you out whenever you bend over or lean down, do you? You know what I think…"

"What's that?" I asked. I did notice, of course, but I never leapt to the conclusion that they all wanted me in bed.

"I think you like playing the cock tease."

I tried to push him away, but Ray held me tight. "Ray!"

"I think it turns you on that the guys want to fuck you." He smiled, like he enjoyed my shocked reaction. Except for when Ian and I role-played recently, I wasn't used to someone talking to me like that. His frankness turned me on.

"I… I…"

Ray did not give me the chance to speak. He kissed me again and his hand slid up my back to unhook my bra, but he couldn't get it done before I pulled his hand away. I may as well have been topless, the bra was translucent in the water, but having some little protection made me feel safer. He pulled me back and went from kissing my neck to kissing my chest and moving lower. Without realizing it, I reacted by grinding into him, and his bulge pressing into my mound sent waves of pleasure through me. I moaned quietly when his lips brushed my nipple through my soaked bra and my nails dug into his shoulders when he nibbled on that tender little morsel. I closed my eyes and gasped his name. Before I knew what was happening, my back was against the hard concrete lip of the pool. I leaned back and rested my arms on it, while Ray kept sucking and nibbling on my breasts. I was so hot that I don't know if I could have handled his lips directly on my skin.

"What are…" I moaned.

I watched him kiss down my tummy as he lifted me so I floated on the surface of the water once again. My knees went over his shoulders and he lightly kissed my thighs. I knew what he wanted to do, but I couldn't let him. Could I? I looked off into the darkness, peering into the greenery surrounding the pool, but I couldn't see Ian there. He just had to be there. How did he feel, watching Ray all over me? And me, letting him he go for it? I was afraid to let things get out of hand, but I also suspected that was exactly what my husband wanted.

"Ray, I don't know…"

He ignored me, as I knew he would. He kissed his way up my thigh and nuzzled my mound through my panties. Just the slightest touch made me jump. God, I was so hot. I was glad for my pool-soaked panties, or he might have known just how much I wanted him. He kissed me through my panties and pressed his face into me. I couldn't help but moan and it encouraged Ray. He held my butt, keeping my pelvis just above the water, and pressed his chin right into my pussy, rubbing right above my clit. My mouth just hung open as I shook and moaned. It was strangely wonderful to be floating in the pool while Ray teased me through my panties. Rubbing back and forth with his chin, he easily brought me to the edge of cumming, then eased off. He waited until my moans died down to a soft whimper, then he sucked on me. Like before, having that sodden, silky barrier between his mouth and my tingling flesh was a delightful tease. I craved his naked touch, but I knew I would lose control if I felt it. I tightened my grip on the edge of the pool and my shaking sent ripples off through the water. I moaned Ray's name, struggling to keep quiet, lest anyone hear us out there. But it was tough and I was losing the battle.

"Nononono…" I pleaded when he pulled my panties to the side. Two fingers filled me, slipping inside so easily, and I cried out. Ray sucked my clit through my panties and fingered me, and just like that I was cumming, crying his name and thrusting my pussy onto his fingers. For the first time in over a decade, a man other than my husband made me cum. I hadn't fucked him, but it was a milestone nonetheless.

When Ray released me, I frantically kissed him and reached under the water, thrusting my hand into his clinging boxer briefs. He felt big and I just barely wrapped my fingers around him. He pushed his underwear off completely and I stroked him under the water. I moved closer and his head nudged me. My panties were plastered to my swollen lips, but thank God they were there because next thing I knew his shaft was between my legs, its length rubbing my lips. I held onto his shoulders while I rocked back and forth. It was as close as we possibly could have come to fucking, and I thought it must be torturing poor Ray. But he let me enjoy myself for a few minutes before leading me out of the pool.

We stood together, kissing and touching, on the concrete, but I didn't notice the chill of the night air on my skin at all. Ray was still bottomless and his prick kept bumping against me, until I grabbed it. I'm sure that made Ian think, but what I did next probably blew his mind.

I sat on the edge of one of those lounges, leaned forward, and kissed Ray's cock. I don't know what got into me. It could have been that I wanted to make him feel good after the orgasm he'd given me, or maybe I wanted to put on a show for Ian out there in the darkness, but I guess the reasons didn't really matter. I put a lot into my performance as I lovingly kissed the flared head and swirled my tongue around it. I squeezed his shaft in my fist and licked up the underside before taking him in my mouth and slowly working my way down. Ray brushed back my wet hair so he had the perfect view of me swallowing him. Inadvertently, he also improved Ian's view. Ray was pretty thick, but he wasn't any longer than average, and I was able to take about three-quarters of him comfortably. There was a time when

I had a lot more practice and could have really gone for it, but I didn't go down on Ian very often anymore.

Ray's balls felt huge when I played with them. I was bobbing up and down, sucking for all I was worth and kneading his balls. I don't know what that does for a guy, but they seem to like it. He really liked watching me sucking him, I knew that. The lustful look in Ray's eyes told me there was nothing on his mind but getting off. He twisted my wet chestnut locks around his fingers and urged me to go faster.

"Dammit Emily…fuck that's good…I fuckin' knew you wanted it…" Ray grunted.

I sucked harder and my cheeks hollowed. He kept saying my name, telling me how good it was, and that only made me want to please him more. I hadn't felt so sexy in years. If he had pushed it just then, I know I would have spread my legs for Ray, not caring how shamed I would feel later. I took all that out on his cock, sucking like I never had before. Soon, he was warning me he was ready.

"I'm gonna cum, baby…fuck it's coming…"

It was sweet of him to warn me, but I wasn't about to stop. Where else was he going to shoot it? On the deck? Ray let out a howl and I thought maybe I'd hurt him, but then he was trembling and his cock jerked in my mouth. Thick, hot cum filled my mouth and I swallowed as fast as I could, but some of it cum bubbled from my lips and dripped onto my chin. *What do you think of your cock-sucking wife now?* I silently asked Ian. It made me so hot to know that I was getting two men off at once.

"Holy shit! Why did we wait to do this until now?" Ray exclaimed after I'd licked him clean.

"Because we shouldn't be doing this at all, I'm a married woman, remember?" I looked down at the wedding ring on my hand when I said it and felt a pang of guilt. I was doing this at my husband's insistence, I reminded myself.

"Right," Ray grinned.

"Speaking of which, I really need to get out of here."

"Sure. I don't want you getting in any trouble, or you may not be allowed out again."

"Let me worry about that. Turn around please."

"Why?"

"Because."

When Ray did as I asked, I shed my bra and pulled on my sweater. I couldn't wear wet underwear beneath my clothing. I knew he stole a peek, but I really didn't mind. After I buttoned my sweater halfway, I stepped into my skirt and pulled down my panties underneath it, giving Ray, who dressed at the same time, a nice flash in the process. I carried my bra and panties in my hand when we left the pool area.

Walking to Ray's car, I spotted Ian's on the far side of the parking lot, but he wasn't in it. He didn't have time to get back to it without being seen. I slid down into the sleek Mercedes, knowing Ian would catch up as soon as he could. Ray gunned the engine and I put my hand over his as he worked the gear shirt. I loved feeling his control over that powerful vehicle. It was the same way he'd been controlling me just a few minutes earlier.

Ray dropped me off at my car and I melted into him, pushing my tongue into his mouth as he pushed his hand under my skirt. There was nothing to stop him from putting his fingers inside me again and I only barely pulled them out. He pressed those fingers to my mouth and I sucked them clean. I'd never done anything like that before! I tasted tangy and sweet and felt so naughty.

"I'll see you tomorrow, baby," he said.

A text awaited me: *See you at home.*

I raced home and found Ian's car parked on the street. The garage door slid up and Ian was like a statue in my headlights. I couldn't read his mood and it started to bother me that I was having so much trouble understanding a man I thought I knew so well. I parked, and as the garage door went down, he came around and opened my door for me.

"Ian, I…"

I truly did not know what to say. For the first time, I did not feel guilty. If I went too far, it was only because I was trying to play his game—and he wouldn't tell me exactly what he wanted. If he liked what he saw, I wasn't sure I was entirely happy with that either. I know he tried to explain, but I still didn't completely understand why he wanted to see me with another man.

"Emily," was all he said.

The garage door closed, and Ian practically ripped the buttons off my sweater pulling it open. He mauled my breasts and I attacked his pants while we kissed in a frenzy. He was like steel and I was still dripping wet. The nanny had to have heard the garage door open and close, but it didn't matter. Ian turned me around and I held onto a metal storage rack and pushed out my ass. He hiked up my skirt and then was in me, fingers digging painfully into my hips. His breath was on my cheek as he bent over me.

"I saw you. I saw it all. I watched you suck his dick," he growled in my ear. He was slamming into me and the rack rattled against the wall.

"You liked that, didn't you? You liked me swallowing his cum…"

"Uhnn…Emmm..yesss…"

"Ohhh…he made me cum…so hard…fuck me! God, fuck me, Ian!"

"Emmm…"

After all that playing with Ray, I needed it so bad. I didn't want to *make love*. I needed to be fucked and that's exactly what Ian did. He took me violently and we both came very quickly. When his spent cock slipped out of me and I turned toward him, we shared a long, deep kiss.

"You know I love you, don't you? I love you so much. Whatever happens with Ray doesn't change that," I said.

"I know, Emily. I've never loved you more than right now."

We exchanged kisses, made ourselves presentable and went inside to a blushing, smiling nanny.

FIVE

IT WAS SO strange to go on as if everything was normal. Ian and I went out to dinner the following night, to have a date of our own, but it was hard to ignore the 800-pound gorilla at the table. I felt like we were making too much of an effort to *not* talk about the game we were playing, when really it was all I wanted to talk about it. Ian may have been content to watch me hook up with Ray and not talk about it, but I was full of conflicting, confused feelings. I really needed someone to talk to. And this was hardly something I was going to discuss with a girlfriend. I could just imagine calling up Fiona and telling her about my hot, younger lover. No, I wanted to talk to Ian about it, but it seemed that the hotter our relationship got sexually, the more he withdrew emotionally.

In the meantime, Ray and I couldn't have been closer. He played it cool at work, but still found a lot of excuses to come by my desk and he insisted we workout together again. The more time I spent with Ray, the more it felt like he really was my boyfriend and not just some casual fling. Getting to know him, I realized he wasn't all swagger and sex, though there was plenty of that. One day, we made out in the elevator on the way back from lunch, and he tried to convince me to go back to his place, but I again dodged his advances. I promised we would get together again. He kept pushing, and I kept putting him off.

I realized I couldn't continue this way. It would be very difficult to keep putting Ray off. We were both adults and I was already fooling around on my husband, so there weren't many excuses left for not going all the way with Ray. Honestly, part of me feared that if I kept putting him off, he would just lose interest. If I kept refusing to be alone with him what else was he going to think? I couldn't tell Ray I wanted him to fuck me, but I needed my husband there to watch us. I wondered if there was a compromise.

I got the idea for what I like to think of as *remote voyeurism* that night watching one of those network newsmagazines. They were doing an exposé and sent one of their producers undercover with a hidden camera into a corrupt business. I wondered, if we had something like that, could Ian watch me and Ray together if we were someplace private? Thinking about the possibilities was exciting, and I grabbed my laptop to do some research.

The myriad ways to spy on someone in this modern age are truly shocking, as I found out with just a few clicks of the mouse. Not only were there endless variations on spy cameras, I found all sorts of devices for capturing computer and cell phone activities and tracking people. Finally, I found just what I needed: a purse with a high resolution video camera sewn into it and a transmitter that would work up to 800 feet away. It came with a receiver that had a seven-inch color screen and a speaker. It seemed perfect.

I considered running downstairs to show Ian, but I just ordered it instead. I wanted it to be a surprise, to show my husband I was just as committed to our game as he was. With rush shipping, we would have it by Friday. I hoped Ian would like the idea, but to be sure, I decided to do a test run and see if Ian liked it.

The following day, Ray and I were scheduled to visit a client together. I was going to be introduced as his replacement and go over the project. It was a morning meeting, and as I always did when meeting clients, I dressed to impress. Early on, a female mentor had taught me that there's nothing wrong with using all your assets as a woman to get ahead. I took her advice to heart, but was always too modest to really show off, until recently.

Since getting into shape after the second pregnancy and becoming more comfortable with my body, I've decided there's nothing wrong with outfits that show off all the work I've put in at the gym. My outfit certainly was not slutty, but the navy skirt was shorter than I might have worn around the office, and the tailored pale pink blouse just hinted at cleavage. I knew Ray approved the second I walked into the office.

After Ray introduced me, I did a brief presentation and I am proud to say that I held his attention for more than my looks. I was confident that I would manage the client with no problems by the time we walked out of the meeting. Ray drove, of course, and we were both in a celebratory mood as we headed back to the office.

"I think that went really well," I said, making sure my skirt was pulled down far enough to hide the lacy tops of my nude stockings. "He was eating out of the palm of my hand."

"I wonder why," Ray smirked, glancing down at my legs.

"What are implying, that he was more interested in my body, than my body of work?" I smiled to show I wasn't offended.

"You didn't see the way he looked at your ass when I showed you into the conference room."

"Ray!" It was nice to know I was still capable of blushing.

"I'm not sayin', I'm just sayin'... With those pumps, your legs and ass look spectacular."

"You just don't want to think anyone can take your place."

"I do bring a special set of skills."

"Is that so?"

"You should know that as well as anyone," he chuckled.

"Ray," I replied, more quietly than before, and turned a deeper shade of red.

"Are we not talking about what happened the other night?" he asked, turning serious. "I don't know about you, but I had a great time."

"I did too. It's just that, you know, all this is new to me. I've never..." I ran my fingers through my hair and looked out the window. I felt him watching. Even with the air conditioning cranked high, it was suddenly hot in the car.

"Never what, Emily? Never gone skinny dipping? Never fooled around in the water? I know you're not saying you've never sucked a guy off before."

Ray touched my leg and his hand crept higher as he spoke. My flesh tingled where he touched me and I closed my eyes, picturing my brazen behavior by the pool. It was exciting to be so bold. As my heart beat faster, I knew I wanted that feeling again.

I smiled and turned to him. "Are you saying I seemed experienced?"

"I'm just saying you were damned good at it."

"Flattery may get you somewhere."

I reached over and touched Ray through his pants just as he moved under my skirt and touched my bare skin. My skirt rode up above my stocking tops when he touched me through my black thong. I spread my legs slightly and sighed when he pressed, running his fingers up and down the cleft between my lips. Suddenly I thought of Ian, and how I shouldn't be doing this if my husband wasn't a part of it. Ray groaned in frustration when I took my hand out of his lap.

"What are you doing?" he asked when I bent forward and

grabbed my phone out of my purse, which was at my feet.

"I just remembered I promised to text Ian and tell him how the meeting went," I said, stifling a moan. Bending forward just pressed his hand harder into my pussy. I texted Ian, warning him: *Answer your phone.*

Before I returned my phone to my purse, I dialed Ian, then muted the volume. He should be able to hear everything that happened in the car. I just hoped Ian was in a position to use his phone.

"This seems like an odd time to be thinking of your husband," Ray smirked, making me jump when he pressed just above my clit.

"You don't want him calling right now, do you?"

I had no idea if Ian got either message, but I just proceeded as if he were listening. I sat back in that luxurious leather seat and opened my legs for Ray. When I reached for him, I found his stiff length running down his right pant leg. I worked to keep him hard while he played with me. I've got to give him credit. He sped down the highway smoothly, despite his distractions. My moisture plastered my thong to my mound and Ray pulled until it was caught between my slick, swollen lips. When he stroked my bare lips, it was amazing.

"Unbutton your top," he demanded.

"But the other cars," I gasped.

"My windows are tinted and no one is looking in anyway. Do it, Emily. I want to see those perfect tits."

I stared at my hands as if they weren't my own, unbuttoned my blouse and pulled it open. My demi-cup bra had a hint of black lace over the cups that pushed me up, just barely covering my nipples. I've always love the way I look in a demi-cup and it appeared that Ray concurred as I felt his cock twitch. I cupped my breast, pushing my nipple out, then rolled the hard nub between my fingers. How did I become so horny so quickly?

"I knew you were a fucking wild cat, baby. You're always ready for some fun, aren't you?" Ray cooed as he massaged my pussy in a rhythm that drove me crazy.

"Ahhh…Ray…yes…your hand on my pussy feels so good."

"You like to talk dirty, don't you?" Ray chuckled.

"Yess, ohhh…Ray…" I'd never thought about it and saying things like that didn't really roll off my tongue, but I was doing it for Ian on the phone as much as for Ray. Was Ian sitting at his desk listening to another man moan and touch me, or had he snuck off to the bathroom?

"Take off your panties, Emily."

I did not even hesitate. I didn't want his hand off of my pussy for a moment longer than was necessary. I slid my thong down my legs and tossed it into my purse. When I sat back, I pulled my skirt up so Ray could see my naked pussy. A lot of guys make the mistake of just shoving their fingers inside you and fucking you with them. But when he put his hand back, he rubbed my slippery lips.

"You know what would make you even hotter?" Ray asked off-handedly.

"What?" I asked, a tremble in my voice. I didn't care much what he asked, as long as he stopped teasing me.

"You should shave everything down below."

"You're one of those guys, are you? You don't like my little landing strip?"

"One of those guys?" His eye brow was arched. He tried to distract me by slipping his fingers between my lips and rubbing my clit. I lifted off the seat as I whimpered, pushing at his fingers.

"I'll think about it," I teased, already wondering what Ian would think if I did as Ray suggested.

I was hot, and Ray expertly brought me right to the edge. He understood just how to touch a woman for maximum pleasure: firm, then light, easing back when it was almost too much, then putting on the gas when I was getting ready to cum. I massaged both my breasts and teased my nipples. My moans filled the interior of the humming German auto.

"Christ you're hot. You've got to let me fuck you, Emily," Ray said, watching me as much as he watched the road.

"Oh Ray…oh Ray…ohhh Rayyyyy…" I moaned over and over. My knuckles were white as I held the door handle in a death grip when I climaxed. Ray made me cum so hard I saw stars when I squeezed my eyes shut, and I think my spiked heel dug almost dug a hole in his floor mat as I ground it down. I was so wet I could hear his fingers on my pussy as he played with me. He could have easily made me cum again if I hadn't pushed his hand away.

"No more…I can't take it…" I breathed. It wasn't a lie. If he didn't stop, I might have demanded he pull over so I could climb on top of him. The more I was with Ray, the harder it was to hold back. I squeezed my thighs shut and I closed my eyes until the shivering stopped. Then I was ready to reward Ray.

"I love making you cum," he said, and licked his sticky fingers clean.

"I love it when you make me cum," I laughed, and leaned over the seat.

While I planted a long hot kiss on him, I reached down and un-buckled his belt. Ray quickly got the idea and his seat glided back. I tasted my tangy sweetness on his breath while we kissed. Reaching into his pants and underwear, I grasped his hot length. Ray switched to cruise control so I could get his pants down and I found a scrunchie in my purse. With my thick, chestnut hair pulled back into a neat po-nytail, I leaned over the center console again, with my butt in the air, and took Ray in my mouth.

I did not play around with him or tease him. I just wanted to get him off, like he'd done for me. I sucked him hard and bobbed rapidly, giving him an intense, quick blowjob. Going down on a guy in the front of a car really took me back. More than one high school and college date ended like this. At least the emergency brake wasn't up and digging into my chest as I leaned across the center console. I noisily slurped as I sucked on him and Ray moaned his appreciation. Could Ian guess at what was going on? Ray would take care of that.

"Christ, you're fucking good. Shit, Em, suck me! You're going to make me fuckin' cum, baby!"

His grip on the back of my neck tightened and he was humping up off the seat into my mouth. I didn't choke but I came close. It was so exciting to go down on him while we hurdled down the highway at seventy miles an hour. The danger rushed through my veins and I wanted Ray inside me more than ever. This game was turning me into someone I hardly recognized. Without any warning but a strangled cry, he came, filling my mouth with his thick, hot cum. I swallowed and swallowed, but it still dripped from my lips and ran down his shaft. When he was finished, I licked him clean and smacked my lips.

"Let's go to a hotel for lunch," Ray grinned.

"I don't think so," I said as I buttoned my blouse. "That will have to hold you for now."

"You are the ultimate fucking tease, Em," he chuckled.

"We'll see," I replied, feeling like I was putting one of my kids off. I reached for my phone as if I were checking for messages and looked at my call log. Ian had been listening the entire time. I'm sure Ray thought my smile was all for him. Oh, to have two men at my leisure!

***

My evening with my husband went as expected after my little escapade in the car. Ian couldn't wait to get the kids to bed and the nanny out of the house so we could be alone. I tortured him by acting as if nothing had happened, deftly sliding away from him every time he tried to pull me in for a kiss. He was downstairs watching SportsCenter while I was upstairs in the shower.

I looked down at my pussy with the razor in my hand and questioned if I really wanted to do this. What was Ian going to think when he saw I was changing to please another man? I bet it would give him a hard-on, which I still did not quite understand. I lathered up and applied the razor in long, clean strokes. Midway through it occurred to me that shaving for Ray turned me on—and not because my husband would like it. I could imagine Ray touching my pussy, telling me how sexy it was, and how he wanted to fuck me more than ever. Does that make me a terrible person?

The warm steel of the blade swept my delicate skin again and again, and when I rinsed I was perfectly clean down there. I touched my smooth flesh and leaned against the cool tiles as a shiver shot through me. I thought about Ray while I rubbed my clit furiously. It had been so long since I'd masturbated, but I couldn't help myself. The ritual of preparing myself for my lover had me so hot. I imagined Ray kissing me down there, pushing my legs back and taking me. In my mind, I wasn't putting him off. I was saying yes I fantasized about Ray filling me with his thick cock and I came hard, biting my fist to stifle my cries. Ian probably couldn't hear me downstairs, but I didn't want to wake the kids.

The second I stepped in front of the television, Ian forgot all about the baseball scores. All I wore was my short kimono robe and my nipples were clear points in the thin silk. I'd only loosely belted the robe, letting it hang open slightly. I wanted Ian to discover my new look on his own.

"So what did you think of my surprise phone call today? I smiled, my face framed by waves of blown-dry hair.

"It was unexpected. I didn't know what was going on... at first." Ian was staring at my body, as if he could make my robe open with sheer willpower. I wasn't sure if he could see what I'd done yet.

"I hope you don't mind that I took some initiative. Ray and I had a great meeting. We were feeling pretty good, and one thing led to another."

"I'd say so! It was awesome, hon. When I figured out what was going on, it was so hot." He was smiling now, too.

Sitting beside him on the couch I took his hand and squeezed it. "What do you think happened?" I leaned back on the couch, just like I had in Ray's Mercedes.

"I know he touched you, but I want you to tell me," Ian said in a low, breathy whisper. He was already excited.

"He just started touching me. He didn't even ask if he could," I said, carefully watching Ian as I touched my pussy with my free hand. My fingers, caressing my lips, hid my freshly-shaven pussy from my husband's eyes.

"And you didn't try to stop him..."

"No, baby, I didn't want to. When Ray starts touching me I get so horny. Mmmm..." Reliving the afternoon, I was just as aroused as I was before I climaxed in the shower.

"He told you to take your panties off." Ian said it eagerly, as if he was picturing it too. Was he imagining himself in the scene, or seeing Ray touching me? I wished I knew.

"Yes, he wanted to touch my naked pussy." It was so strange how talking dirty came so naturally to me now, but I wanted to be dirty for Ian. I knew that's what he wanted from me, and I wanted to make his fantasies come true.

"I took off my thong and stuffed it in my purse, then he touched me again."

This was the moment of truth. I placed Ian's hand over my mound, and as soon as he felt my clean, wet lips, his eyes widened. He was excited when he spoke, but there was something else too, something darker.

"You did what he wanted," he said simply.

"Yesss… oh baby, touch me, please," I moaned.

"You're so smooth." It sounded like he couldn't believe it.

"Ohhh, baby, do you like it?" I cooed.

"It feels so different…yes…honey…yes…"

Ian had trouble getting his words out, and I started rubbing him through his shorts just as I'd touched Ray. My husband was rock-hard, and I was so excited know that I was the reason. While I kept one hand on his cock, my other was still guiding Ian's hand on my pussy. I wanted him to touch me just like Ray did. He got the hang of it and when he really focused on my clit, I felt my orgasm coming on fast.

"He…he…rubbed my pussy…just like that…Iann…" I moaned.

"He made you cum, didn't he?"

"Yesss…yesssss…YES!" I cried, hitting a fantastic peak. My body jackknifed off the couch and I grabbed him hard. My pussy was flowing and Ian fingers slid all over my swollen red lips. Ian rolled to his side and kissed me, thrusting his tongue into my mouth and slammed two fingers into me hard and quick. I heard my sex squishing around those digits. It kept my orgasm going until I pushed Ian back. I wanted more than his fingers.

"Do you know what I did after he made me cum?" I asked, getting up on my knees on the couch and shedding my robe. I brushed his face with my breast and he captured my nipple, making me moan while he sucked on the tingling little nub.

"You blew him," Ian said flatly.

"Did you mind me sucking his cock?" I asked, wanting to make it sound dirty. I freed Ian's prick and stroked it up and down.

"No….fuck you're hot, Emily…oh God…"

His words strangled off when I took him in my mouth. He aggressively pushed on the back of my head and thrust his hips, fucking my mouth. My husband had never been like that, but I guess the mood took over. I tried to relax, but it was difficult to keep from choking.

"Ahhh…suck it…suck it you hot cocksucker…" Ian grunted. I couldn't believe what was coming from him.

I wanted to make Ian feel good, but I also wanted to have sex with him. God, I needed him inside me. I felt his cock swell in my mouth and I tried to pull away, but he held me in place. When I did finally free myself, it was too late. Ian's thick cum blasted right in my face, coating my cheeks and dripping from my nose. I looked like a gooey mess when I finally pulled away. Ian stared at me with a thoroughly alien look. What was he thinking? It was like he'd lost all control.

"Are you okay?" I asked, wiping my face with a throw blanket on the back of the sofa. "Are *we* okay?"

"Yeah…yeah," he said hurriedly, and looked away.

"Ian, look at me. Are we okay?"

He looked into my eyes, but I could tell it took effort. "Yes, we're okay. I guess I just got carried away," he said sheepishly.

"If this game with Ray is too much, I want you to tell me. We can stop this all right now."

"No!" He blurted out. "No, I don't want to stop. I'm sorry if I got too rough."

I smiled and shyly looked away. "I kind of liked it, actually. Your passion was hot."

"Really?"

"Really, it was. I have to admit, I like the way you've been looking at me since we started *playing*. God, I must look like a mess right now." I used my fingers to wipe some of the remaining cum from my cheek and rubbed it between my fingers. With Ian watching closely, I licked my fingers clean.

"A hot mess," he laughed.

"Oh? You like seeing me with your cum on my face?" I looked down and saw he was already half-hard again. I must say, I was very pleased with how this all was affecting his recovery time. I grasped him and started pumping his shaft.

"It's like I'm watching you transform before my eyes," he breathed. He was almost ready.

"Into what?" I wasn't sure I wanted to hear the answer, no matter how hot it might make me.

"I..."

I didn't give him the chance to answer. I straddled Ian and took him right up inside me. He held onto my butt and I leaned back, holding onto his shoulders. This was no slow lovemaking. There wasn't even dirty talk. I tried not to think of Ray, and rode Ian hard while he pulled me into him. He stared at me like he'd just met me. I came again, but Ian lasted much longer. If not for my quickie in the shower I might have cum with him again, I loved it when we did that, but I couldn't quite manage. Maybe there were too many conflicting thoughts in my head. When my husband finally came, I was happy to finally climb down and rest. We were both sweaty, and I would need another shower before bed, but it was well worth it.

SIX

ALONE INSIDE ONE of the videoconference suites at my office, I smiled into the camera as I untied my sea-green silk wrap blouse at my hip and pulled it open. Underneath was a hunter green demi-cup bra, with thin, wide straps and a little bow in the middle, like I was a present waiting to be unwrapped. I liked the blouse because the low neckline suggested cleavage without actually showing it. That made it perfect for the office, and Ray. I know he was thinking exactly what I wanted him to, because he looked very disappointed when I turned him down for lunch earlier in the day.

But at that moment, I was speaking to my husband.

"I'm doing this for you, honey, so I hope you enjoy the show."

On a video monitor next to the camera, I could see Ian looking back at me, sitting on our bed, wearing a t-shirt and shorts. His laptop was on the mattress beside him. In the background I could hear the kids somewhere in the house. Presumably, the nanny was taking care of them while Ian was busy and I was "working late."

Ian was hungry for whatever I had planned. It was written all over his face. He looked like he was waiting for the Super Bowl to start. "What are you up to? Where are you?" he asked.

"I'm in the teleconference room," I answered. He knew I had done remote presentations as part of my job. "Just about everyone's left for the day and no one knows I'm here."

I neatly folded my blouse and laid it aside. Next, I unsnapped my snug, charcoal slacks and peeled them down. I knew both Ray and Ian loved the way my butt looked in them. My lace-trimmed boy shorts matched my bra. I had to step out of my three-inch heels to pull the slacks off, but then I stepped back into them.

"*No one* knows you're there?" Ian asked knowingly, and eagerly waited for my answer.

"Well, *someone* knows I'm here. I told him to meet me, and he should be around any minute now. I'd better turn off the monitor."

Before I did, I took a good look at my own image in the small window on the screen to make sure I had a good idea of what the camera would catch. It was one of those fancy ones on a swivel, and was designed to track movement and follow whoever was speaking. The conference table was large enough for about five people to comfortably sit, and the camera was set to capture anything from the tabletop and up. While I was standing, it caught me from just below my butt. I picked up the remote to switch off the monitor. It wouldn't do to have Ray come in and see that my husband was set up to watch us.

"Wait," he said, hurriedly. I saw something besides lust in his eyes. Was it concern? "I love you," he said.

"I love you too, honey. See you when I get home." I switched off the monitor and reached into my purse, which was on the seat at the head of the table. I dug out the roll of black electrical tape I took from Ian's tool box. After tearing off a small piece, I stuck it over the red light on the active camera. Yes, I thought of everything. The camera tracked my movements as I went back to the head of the table and took a deep breath. Hopefully Ray would be too distracted to notice the camera moving if we moved beyond its range. I was ready.

Although I was expecting it, the three sharp raps on the door made me jump. That was the signal that it was Ray. I was suddenly nervous and questioned if this was a good idea. I wanted to put on another show for Ian and thought this would be a good way to do it, to test if being a video voyeur was satisfying for him. I thought I had all my bases covered: The office was empty, Ian was set up, and now here was Ray, but I couldn't help worrying. We could still be discovered and that would be the end of my job. But I was so excited, it was easy to push that fear aside.

I unlocked the door and opened it a crack, while hiding behind it. I peeked out and saw Ray waiting. "What's with all the cloak and dagger?" he asked.

"I just thought it would be fun to get together and this seemed like a safe place. No windows, locking doors, it's after hours."

"We could have just gone to my place," he chuckled, squeezing through the gap. I pushed the door closed and locked it again behind him. "Goddamn!" Ray exclaimed when he got a good look at me. "I wasn't expecting this." He tried to pull me close, but I pushed him back.

"I hoped it would be a nice surprise," I said, smiling seductively. I couldn't believe how comfortable I was standing nearly naked in front of Ray. There was no blushing, no stammering. I was in full control of my sexual power.

"You can say that again. Damn, Emily, you're full of fucking surprises."

"I guess you just bring it out in me." I sat on the edge of the table, aware that Ian would have a great side view of us, and reached for Ray. "Come here and kiss me hello."

Ray pounced, running his fingers through my hair and pushing his tongue into my mouth. I fumbled with the buttons on his shirt and his hands massaged down my back to grab my ass and lift me off the table. I wrapped my legs around him and he held me up while kissing and nibbling my neck.

"I thought you were having second thoughts after you blew me off earlier," he breathed between kisses.

"I was just saving it all for now. You can't have everything you want, whenever you want it, baby. You can't always be in control," I moaned.

I felt so sexy that this hot younger guy couldn't wait to get his hands on me. I wished I could have bragged to my girlfriends. Ray had no idea how hard it was to turn him down earlier. After yesterday, I was like a new woman. I don't know if it was playing with Ray in the car, or the quick, aggressive sex with my husband -- maybe both -- but I woke up that morning hornier than ever. I wanted a morning quickie, but Ian was already in the shower and there was just too much to do before work. I was so tempted to tell Ian what I was planning, but I wanted it to be a surprise for him too. I sent him an email in the middle of the afternoon with instructions for how to log in to the video conferencing system. All that anticipation did a number on me, and I was wet before Ray ever even touched me.

"I don't mind when a woman takes charge," Ray said, nibbling on my neck.

"Careful," I chided. "Don't leave any marks for me to explain to my husband."

"I'll try to return you in one piece."

Ray sat me back on the table and I pushed his shirt off. He really was in terrific shape and I ran my hands all over his chest, mapping the lines of his muscles and tracing his six-pack. I leaned in and kissed his chest, following where my fingers had just been on his warm, smooth skin. My tongue flicked his nipple and he tensed and moaned. When I sucked, his fingers tightened in my hair and he let me suck until he couldn't take, and then moved me to his other nipple. He was taking back control, but I liked how he directed me. All I wanted to do was please my young lover. He pulled my face back to his, and I snaked my tongue out before our lips even met. I knew that would drive Ian crazy. As much as I wanted to please my lover, I wanted to be the dirty girl my husband needed just as badly.

"Mmmm, Ray," I moaned when he grabbed both of my breasts, mashing them in his hands and finding my stiff nipples through the soft cups of my bra. He pinched and rolled them until I was quivering and moaning uncontrollably, and I reached back to unhook my bra. He pulled it away and threw it blindly, almost hitting the camera. His thumbs teased my naked nipples and I arched my back, pushing at him.

"Wait…wait…" I whimpered, pushing his hands away. It took every ounce of self-control to stop him. I needed to cool down or I was going to be in trouble. I had no idea doing it in the office, with my husband watching, would get me so insane. This was my hottest encounter with Ray so far. I slid off the table and turned him around. When he sat on the edge, I pushed him back and pulled off his pants.

I did a quick wink for the camera and leaned forward over the table to kiss Ray's erection. I swept the hair out of my face and pulled it all to the right side as I held his prick and ran my tongue around the head. Ian would have the best look ever at me going down on Ray. After licking the head clean, I took it in my lips and sucked hard, while fluttering my tongue. Ray gasped my name while he leaned up on his elbows to watch me sucking him. My eyes locked on his and I slipped more and more of him into my mouth. Lips stretching around his impressive girth, I took almost all of him before I had to stop. I held the base and wetly sucked him while moaning around my mouthful. What must Ian think seeing me act so wantonly! I couldn't wait to get home and see his reaction. I pulled back and let Ray's head go with a loud pop. I smiled and licked him from base to tip, working my tongue vigorously like, I was trying to get the last of the icing from an egg beater.

"Holy shit, Em! You are the hottest fucking thing I've ever seen. Ohhh, fuck, baby…"

His shaft was slick with my saliva and I stroked it as I kept licking, making sure I had his full attention. From the look on his face, I thought he might cum any second. Kicking it up a notch, I started licking his balls, then sucking them. I didn't even do that for Ian, but I wanted to be as dirty as I could be. This was my show, and I had to give it my all.

"Fuck…shit…you're sucking my balls! You're sucking my fucking balls, Emmm…"

Ray's stating of the obvious made me suck his balls harder. He did a good job of manscaping, so it wasn't so bad down there, but I was ready to get back to the main attraction. I ran my tongue up the underside of his shaft and took him back in my mouth. This time, Ray, ever-thoughtful pulled my hair back, not knowing he had given my husband a good look at me bobbing on his cock. I sucked him hard and fast and Ray pumped his hips up from the table to meet my mouth. I almost gagged, but I didn't slow down. I wanted to make him blow his load, and for my husband's benefit, I wanted him to do it all over my face. Ray held my head in both hands and I thought it was to fuck my mouth, but he actually pulled me back. I couldn't believe it! I knew he was going to cum.

"You're not getting off that easy tonight, Em," Ray huffed, sitting up and hopping down from the table. He lifted me and put me in his spot.

"But…" I weakly protested. Things were rapidly going sideways.

We kissed and Ray pushed me onto my back on the table. It was smooth and hard on my back, but warmed from Ray having been there. When he leaned over me to kiss my breasts I was all too aware of how close his cock was to my sex. Thank God I was still wearing my panties. I should have pushed him back, moved him off of me, but I couldn't. I didn't want to. He was sucking on my nipples, drawing them out, while lashing them with his tongue, and I was in heaven. Our two video conferencing rooms are lightly soundproofed, luckily for me, because I was getting loud as he went from side to side, licking and sucking and nibbling on me. I massaged the back of his neck, while his hands slid down and held my hips. The scalding tip of his cock bobbed against my thighs, and all I could think about was how close we were to having sex.

"Mmmm…Ray…oohhh…baby…sooo good…*please*…" I didn't even know what I was pleading for.

His fingers hooked in the waistband of my boy shorts. They slid down over my butt and past my thighs.

"Ray…noooo…we can't…"

Ray ignored me and my panties were gone. He kissed down my trembling, flat belly and nuzzled my bare pussy. He smiled and said, "Did you do this for me?"

"I…I…"

He kissed my pussy, softly probing between my lips with his tongue. "Did you?"

"Yesss…Ray…"

Ray took my *yes* as permission to proceed, and honestly, I did nothing to stop him. He spread my lips open and explored me with his tongue, turning my whimpers to uncontrolled moans. He was just so amazing with his tongue and fingers. He massaged my mound while kissing it and roamed with his tongue, building me quickly to a climax, but backing away before I got there. He teased my clit incessantly and I begged him to let me cum. I just didn't care how it looked. Ray had total control of my body.

"Rayyy…Rayyy…*please*…ohhhhh…*please!*"

Two fingers entered me and I thrust my pussy at them, eager for the invasion. He sucked my clit while I fucked his fingers and I was gone. I cried out loudly and my fists hammered the table as I came, crying Ray's name and pushing myself at him. He noisily slurped my juices and I thought I was going to cum again when he pulled back. My eyes were closed and I was in a world all my own. I only caught him at the very last second.

My legs were open wide and bent in the air, making it all too easy for him. The warm flesh pressing my slick lips was not his fingers. My eyes snapped open and I looked down to see him standing over me, his cock in his hand and teasing me.

"Ray! No!" I cried. I tried closing my legs, but he was already between them. I had no escape. His thick head ran up and down my cleft and my head swam. It would be so easy to just let him put it in.

"Cut the shit, Em. I know you want it. It's all over your face. I know you want to fuck me," he smirked.

"Ray, no. I can't…my husband…"

"If you were so worried about your husband you wouldn't be here with me."

His head brushed my clit and I jumped, moaning. "I just can't, Ray. Please! Anything else…" I pleaded. The head was practically between my lips. I hoped that with my leg bent, Ian couldn't see. "Please…"

"I'm not going to rape you, but I don't believe you don't want it," Ray huffed. He loosened his grip on my thigh and pulled his cock back, leaving a sticky web trailing back to my pussy.

I scrambled up to the edge of the table and grabbed him. I was so desperate not to lose him. I didn't want to disappoint him, but he had to understand I was a married woman. I had my limits. How could I make him understand?

"Ray, I'm sorry."

"I'm not some toy for you to tease, Em. We're not going to keep doing this if you're not serious. I want that sweet little pussy of yours, and you wouldn't be here if you didn't want to give it to me. Just let go."

I grabbed his cock, holding him there. He was still essentially between my legs. I could just pull him forward, put him inside me. He was right. I did want to fuck him, right there on the table. But that was too far. How could I be *that* woman? As much fun as I was having, I was doing it to put on a show for my husband. It wasn't just about me and what I wanted, and I couldn't believe Ian actually wanted me to fuck someone else.

"I'm sorry. I'm not trying to tease you. There are other ways I can make you feel good," I forced a smile and stroked his cock. I was genuinely upset that I let Ray down. How had his feelings come to matter to me so much?

"You give a great blow job, but I want more. I want it all."

"I don't know what to say."

Ray pulled me off of the table and pushed me to my knees. The table was even with my chin and I didn't know what Ian could see. Ray pulled me back by my hair and fed me his cock. I opened and sucked him avidly. He was in total control and I just sucked as he pulled me back and forth on his cock and used my mouth. He grunted like an animal. It was just like it had been with Ian the night before, and it made me so hot. I reached down and rubbed my clit while Ray used my mouth. I easily brought myself to another orgasm and I came at the same time as Ray. He flooded my mouth, and his thick cum ran down my chin as I tried to swallow and moan at the same time. His cock slipped from my mouth and it wiped it across my lips. He still looked angry, but he was also satisfied.

"I don't know if you're playing some kind of game with me, but game time is over, Em. I like you a lot, but we're both adults here and we know how these things go. You can't play the virginal waif with me. Don't keep going down this road if you're not ready for where it leads. I want you, and I'll be here when you're ready."

"Ray...Ray..."

He ignored me as he pulled on his pants and then his shirt, which wasn't even fully buttoned when he left. Ray left me on my knees in the teleconference room, with his cum on my face while I stared at the door. I was in shock. It wasn't supposed to go like this. I felt numb as I stood up and leaned forward to turn off the camera.

***

"It's over, Ian! I can't do this again!" I exclaimed, trying to keep my voice down because I didn't want to wake the kids. The house was mostly dark when I came in. I planned on composing myself before I went upstairs to face Ian, maybe have a glass of wine to steel my nerves, but I had found him waiting for me in the kitchen.

"Emily, honey, try to calm down," he said, standing up from his chair and crossing the room to meet me. He tried to hold me, but I just pushed him away.

I turned away and tried to compose myself. It was a relief to come home and find that Ian had sent the nanny home early and already had the kids in bed. I don't think I could have faced anyone. I looked normal enough, I cleaned up in the ladies room at work before

I left, but I was in turmoil. Ian put his hands on my shoulders from behind.

"Ian, I'm sorry about tonight. I didn't plan on that happening. Oh God…" I was barely fighting back the tears.

"Don't be sorry. I thought you were amazing tonight. That was so hot. I can't believe you did that for me!"

I turned, blinking away my tears when I looked my husband in the eyes. He wasn't upset at all. In fact, he seemed positively giddy. Didn't he realize how close I'd come to fucking another man?

"But…at the end…I almost…didn't you see…" I don't know how much sense I was making. It was like I was suddenly in a bizarre universe and my brain didn't want to work.

"Emily, everything was great. I don't understand what you're so upset about. You were incredible tonight." He tried to take my hands, but I didn't want to be touched. I didn't know what I wanted.

"Ian. What are you doing? Why aren't you upset?"

"How can I be upset? Tonight was everything I've wanted. I know you liked it to, like you told Ray. Why are you upset?" He leaned back against the table.

Guilt was turning to anger, and it flared inside me, erupting like a volcano. "I almost fucked another man! Is that okay with you? Is that what you really want?"

"Emily…"

"Is it? Was that the plan? Do you want to watch me fuck someone else?"

Ian grabbed for me and I tried to push him away, but he latched onto my arms and wasn't letting go.

"What the fuck, Emily? You set up this whole thing up today, not me! Don't pretend this has all been about me. I see how you are with him. I know that you want Ray."

I stammered instead of speaking, because I didn't know what to say, unless I was going to lie. Ian may have started all this, but he didn't have to twist my arm to keep going. I was a full participant now. More than that, I was an instigator. My husband may have prodded me into my first date with Ray, but Ian didn't ask me to go down on Ray in the car. And I planned my performance this evening all on my own. As I realized what I hypocrite I was, I deflated and sagged against Ian. My anger was not entirely abated. I felt there was more to this than he'd ever told me. I never intended to go as far as sleeping with another man, but now I was sure that was Ian's endgame.

"Don't you see how dangerous this is? How wrong it is?"

He brushed the hair back from my face. "I don't see anything wrong. All I see is how sexy you are and how this experience has made our marriage hotter than it's been in years. Why do you want to stop now?"

"Because I'm afraid things will go too far!" I shouted.

Ian's lips twisted into a cruel smile. "I don't think you're afraid things will go too far. I think you're afraid because you *want* them to go too far."

"What?" I acted outraged, but his words pierced my heart, because deep down I feared he was right. I didn't understand how that couldn't make me angry. I turned my back to him once again and he held me by the hips. I looked back at him over my shoulder.

"You're not mad at me. You're mad at yourself, because you want this as much as I do," he said. His hands slid up my body, cupping my breasts. I could have told him to stop, that I didn't want it, but my long nipples were already peaking to hardness and he would have known I was lying.

Before I could refute his accusations, Ian turned me and kissed me hard. I had no choice but to return his kiss. He'd never kissed me like that. Anger and passion and control raged in his kiss. My mouth opened and his tongue speared into it, invading me. Even while I kissed him back, I struggled against his hold, but that just seemed to make him hold me tighter. I didn't want this. I was angry and scared and the last thing on my mind was having sex with my husband.

Or was it? Ian's passion ignited my own. I stopped struggling and pulled Ian into me. My guilty heart admitted he was right. I did want things to go too far with Ray. To be blunt, I wanted him to fuck me. But I couldn't say that out loud. I couldn't say I wanted to cheat on my husband.

We clawed at each other's clothing, pulling and tearing. I easily stripped Ian's t-shirt off, but he had more trouble with my top. He had no patience and I heard ripping as he tore my blouse free and peeled it off of me. My pussy clenched as I thought about Ian taking me. He turned me around and roughly pushed me down over the kitchen table. He yanked my pants down and my panties went with them. I heard his shorts tumble against the hardwood floor and felt the hot tip of his tool bouncing against my butt.

"Oh God, Ian!" I cried out when he stabbed his cock into me. There was no warning, no making sure I was ready for him. He just shoved it inside me and found me dripping wet. "Oh God, yes!"

"You're so fucking hot, Em. I don't want to stop! I don't want to go back to before!" Ian grunted.

"God…Ian…don't stop…"

Ian slammed me so hard, it was like he was trying to drive his prick right through me. I tried to get up, but he just shoved me back down like I was just some whore there for his pleasure. Maybe I was just then. His hand stayed between my shoulder blades, keeping me pinned to the hard, cool wood of the kitchen table. I twisted my head just enough to look back at him. His expression was primal, almost like he wasn't even there. Was he even seeing me, or was he just fucking? I feared he was seeing something else.

"You want to fuck him, don't you?" Ian growled.

"Ian..." I pleaded. I knew what he saw. My husband was picturing me fucking another man and it made his cock surge inside me.

"Say it! Tell me you want to fuck him!"

"Ian...I...I..."

I couldn't answer him because suddenly my mind went where his already was. Ray was so close to taking me at work. His cock was almost inside me. What if he hadn't been so wonderful? If he was like every other man, he would have just taken me right on that table. He knew I wanted it, just as my husband did. *I'm not going to rape you*, Ray said. It wouldn't have been, even if he'd taken me violently the way Ian did now. I may have told him no when he started, but before long I would have been begging him. I would have been screaming, "Yes!"

"Yes!" I howled. "I want to fuck Ray! Ohhh...is that what you want to hear?"

"Em...tell me...TELL ME..."

"I want him! I wanted to fuck him today...I wanted him inside meee...God...I want his cock!"

"Uhhnnn...Em..."

"Fuck me! Fuck me, Ian... Don't stop!"

Ian pounded me faster and faster, and his hand moved to my head, holding it down on the table so I couldn't look at him. I closed my eyes and the darkness filled with obscene images of Ray taking me from behind. How were we not waking the kids? How were we not waking the neighbors?

"Tell me...say it..." Ian growled into my ear. Sweat dripped from his forehead onto my cheek.

"Fuck me…fuck me…fuck me, Ray! Fuck me Ray!"

"Uhhnnnn…Em…"

"Come on, baby…cum with meee…cum…with…meeee…"

I pushed my butt at him, thrusting against Ian as I felt him explode, blasting deep inside me. It triggered my own orgasm and the world spun around me. For just a second, I was on that table and it was Ray who was on top of me, making me cum. God help me, but I wanted that. I wanted to know what it was like to make love to Ray.

Ian stayed on top of me, keeping me pinned to the table. His spent cock was still inside me and I wanted to keep it there.

"You really do want to fuck him, don't you?" He whispered in his ear. His voice was full of love, but there was something else there too, something I couldn't understand. Did he hate me for what I said?

"I don't know what to say, Ian." I finally pushed up from the table , forcing Ian off of me, and found my blouse. I pulled it on, but I didn't tie it closed.

"Say you'll do it."

"What?" I asked, paused in the middle of pulling my hair back into a ponytail. I wasn't expecting that.

"I know you want to fuck Ray and I want to see you do it, so finally just admit the truth."

"You really want me to sleep with another man?" I asked carefully, twisting my hair to stay in place.

Ian smirked. "I doubt there will be much sleeping."

I punched him in the arm. "This is no time to be funny. You're saying you really want to see me having sex with Ray?"

"I think this is something we all want, even Ray, if his feelings matter to anyone."

"But I don't think I can. It's going too far…"

"Is it really? I think you're just rationalizing. You've sucked his cock. He's gone down on you." His words stung. I felt like such a jezebel. "We all want this, so it's silly to pretend we don't."

"Maybe I am rationalizing, but it doesn't feel right."

"None of this felt right in the beginning, did it?"

"No."

"But then you gave yourself to the experience and you've loved every second. So why deny yourself the ultimate indulgence?"

He was so eager, like this was the only thing he wanted in the world. It's crazy, but I started to feel like I'd be letting my husband down if I refused to sleep with another man. Did morality even matter anymore? It reminded me of high school, when I would go down on a boyfriend to keep from sleeping with him. I told myself then that I was maintaining my virginity, but it was just a technicality.

I knew now that I couldn't stand on morality anymore. I'd already given myself to Ray in every way that mattered. And I did enjoy it. So really, why shouldn't I have sex with Ray? The only reason would be because it would hurt Ian—but he wanted me to! He wanted to share me with another man. To my dying day, I would never understand why he wanted this, but I was playing along, wasn't I?

"So you really want this?" I asked warily.

"Yes. So do you," he insisted.

"Yes, I want to have sex with Ray, but I could live without doing it. I'll do it, but I want you to understand, I am doing this for you. I'm going to fuck Ray, and I know I'll enjoy it, but I am going to do it for you."

The dark cloud I'd seen so many times crossed his face again, but then he smiled. "Okay."

And so it was decided. I was going to fuck another man while my husband watched. And if I was going to do this, I was going all in. I was going to enjoy Ray every way I wanted, and I would put on the ultimate show for my husband. I just hoped we could put it all behind us afterward.

SEVEN

IT TURNED OUT that deciding to have sex with Ray was the easy part. Figuring out how to make it happen was difficult. After my freak out in the teleconference room, I didn't know how I was going to face him, let alone tell him I was ready for it all. It was like when I got a bad grade on a test and dreaded having to bring it home for my father's signature. The dread kept building until it was paralyzing. Of course, going to Ray would have happier outcome, I was sure. He wasn't likely to punish me. Or was he? That could actually be fun.

When I first went in the following morning, I headed straight for my cubicle like a woman on a mission. I stared straight ahead, fearing I might catch Ray's eye, and moved so swiftly I nearly knocked over one of the interns. I sat in my cubicle with that crawling feeling between my shoulder blades, like I was waiting for a shot from some unseen sniper that never came. No emails or instant messages awaited me, and I wondered if I'd teased Ray for the last time. If he'd decided he was done with me, maybe it was just as well. I could go to Ian and tell him that Ray wasn't interested anymore and that we were done playing. Things could go back to normal and I could have my life back.

As much as I enjoyed playing the vamp, it just didn't feel right to me. I didn't think I had it in me to be some kind of crazy swinger. The fantasy of having two men at my beck and call was exciting, but the reality was exhausting. I just didn't know what to do with all my conflicting emotions. I know Ian just saw Ray as my plaything—a means to an end—but it was hard for me to just think of him as a piece of meat, even if he was a very appealing piece of meat. I liked Ray, and I had to keep myself in check to avoid developing real feelings for him. It was one of the reasons I was afraid to sleep with him. What if the sex was mind blowing? Combine that with our chemistry, and there was the danger I'd have trouble letting Ray go. Ian didn't seem concerned about that, but for me, this wasn't just sex. Real feelings were involved. It was why I felt like I was cheating with Ray, even if I had my husband's full permission. But if I was going to go forward, I had to bury that. I had to find my inner slut and just make it all about the pleasure.

Lunchtime came and went and there was still no sign of Ray, although I did skip the gym to avoid him. He could have called out sick, but I didn't want to ask anyone. I knew that our recent behavior was drawing unwanted attention, and I didn't want to appear to be curious about his whereabouts. I finished up my work for the day, relieved that I hadn't seen Ray. If only relief was all I felt. I'd being lying if I didn't admit to being a little disappointed too. I didn't want things to end with Ray this way. Deep down, I wanted to see my boy-toy again, no matter how much I protested to Ian.

Waiting for the elevator, I was convinced that Ray never came in when, out of the blue, as if I'd conjured him from my mind, he appeared right beside me. Seeing me startle, Ray smiled and touched me on the shoulder.

"How was your day? Did you get much done?" he asked innocently.

"I guess so. How about you? I thought you were out today."

"I was just chained to my desk. There's a lot to get done before I leave, and I've been a little distracted the last few days." He grinned meaningfully.

"About that...we really should talk."

"Do we have something to talk about?"

"I hope so," I replied. The elevator dinged and we stepped into it by ourselves. I hit the button for the lobby.

"I'm sorry if I was rough on you last night, but come on, Emily, what are we playing at here? I'm all for fooling around, but I'm not looking for a high school girlfriend."

"I can't be your girlfriend. I'm married," I replied quickly.

What would it have been like to be Ray's girlfriend back in high school? It wasn't quite so long ago for him, was it? It was funny how little I knew about him, considering the time we'd been spending together. But then, we weren't talking much when we were with each other. I had a feeling that if I was his girlfriend in high school, I would have spent a lot of time in the backseats of cars, or in my basement. The basement was always my location of choice to fool around with boys. The backs of cars were too uncomfortable and my parents would foolishly leave us to our own devices, as long as we left the door at the top of the stairs open. We'd put on a movie and then we'd be all over each other. The stairs were creaky, so there was plenty of warning if my mother decided to come down and do a load of laundry. Back then, I could get my clothes back on in seconds, even if it meant my bra was crammed under the sofa cushions.

"I know that. You know what I mean. I can't pretend that I don't want to fuck you. Christ, it's all I think about these days," Ray said.

"Really?" I don't know why that surprised me, but it did and I blushed a bit.

"Of course. Don't tell me it's not on your mind too."

"It is," I admitted. Maybe I didn't think about it as much as Ray did—or even Ian—but I did think about giving myself to my younger lover. I craved to know what it would be like to give myself to him fully, but I was scared. "It's just that I have so much to lose."

The elevator door opened and we both said goodnight to the guard in the lobby as we passed. Ray held the door and we were on the sidewalk. His parking garage was in the opposite direction of the train station. I stared up into his dark eyes and wondered what my next move was. Did I just put it out there and tell him I was ready? I had to conjure the woman I was in the teleconference room, but it was difficult, because now I knew how this would end. I couldn't claim naiveté and run away this time. I took his hand and asked if he could give me a ride home.

We walked to his car in silence and he held the door while I slid into it. I was going to miss riding in that powerful luxury coupe. It really was the perfect car for Ray: sleek, handsome and powerful. I ran my fingers over the polished wood trim on the dashboard, the way I loved to touch his smooth, hard chest. He joined me in car and I turned in my seat and took both his hands. With the tinted windows, it was dark sitting in the car in the parking garage. Intimate.

"I want this, Ray. I do. I want you. But you have to understand, I still love my husband. This can't ever be anything more than what it's been—two people having fun."

"I get it. You love him, but there's something you're not getting at home."

"I…" I wanted to correct him, but maybe he wasn't wrong. I thought everything was perfect with Ian before all this, but was if it really was, would we be doing this? Would I be doing this? My sex life with Ian had always been great, but was there something missing? I've had some deep, dark fantasies, every woman does. But that doesn't mean we ever seriously consider fulfilling them. Maybe I was different. Was I the woman who—given the chance—would risk everything to fulfill some dark desire? It certainly seemed that way.

"You don't have to explain yourself. I know what you need. I can see it written all over you, in your eyes and the way you move, the way you started dressing the last few months. You were a woman looking for attention, and now that you have it, you're scared. I get that. But I don't want to take anything you don't want to give. I'm not looking to tear your family apart. I just want to enjoy you in the short time we have."

"I want that, too," I admitted. "I want to let go with you, like yesterday, but then the fears come. I don't want to be a slut." I looked away, unable to meet his eyes, because I knew that's exactly what I was.

"You're not a slut. Trust me, I've known some," he grinned.

"I bet you have," I chided, glad for the tension breaker.

"Listen, you're a woman with strong sexual needs and you've decided to indulge yourself. You're not out picking up men in clubs. You're with one guy, and I'm glad that guy is me."

"Me too." I leaned across and kissed him. I'd meant it to be sweet, but Ray held the back of my neck, caressing with those wonderful fingers, and I opened my mouth to him. Every kiss with him was electrifying.

"We could go to my place right now," he suggested.

I pressed my forehead to his and sighed. It was tempting, but nothing was set-up. And I wanted time to prepare myself mentally. I needed to get back to where I was on our dates. "I can't, not tonight."

"Come over this weekend, then. I have a couple friends helping me pack, which will give you an excuse to come over, and after they leave, we can be together." He kissed me again and I leaned further across the seat. Ray palmed my breast, lightly touching me and raising my nipple through my thin silk blouse and bra.

"Okay," I said breathlessly.

"Are you sure you're ready for this, Em?"

"I am," I replied, and decided to show him just how serious I was.

I unfastened his belt and he helped pull his pants down. Here I was, getting more action in cars in my thirties than I had as a teenager. I liked that it felt dirty and wrong. When I told Ray I was afraid of becoming a slut, it was true, but not totally for the reasons he guessed. I was also scared that I enjoyed it too much. I had his cock out and took it right in my mouth. Ray rubbed my back and effortlessly unhooked my bra through my blouse. I swallowed him deeply and hummed into his prick when he reached beneath me and groped my breasts. I loved the way it felt when he pinched my nipples through the silk of my blouse, but I pushed his hand away. I wanted this to be about him, and proving that I wanted him. I was getting very wet, but I would take care of that later. Maybe I would even have Ian fuck me while I told him about this blowjob. I knew that would get us both off.

"Fuck, Em...fuck that's good..." Ray moaned, stroking my hair and letting me work at my own pace. I know he wanted to just ram it into my mouth. I admired his restraint. Ray's control was one of the sexiest things about him. I stroked his saliva-slick cock while I sucked on his balls, something I now knew he loved. He shook and his fingers tightened in my hair when I took him back into my mouth. I really poured it on, sucking hard while I bobbed on his shaft and used my tongue the entire time. He couldn't hold out long against that, and soon he filled my mouth. I swallowed the thick load and smacked my lips when I released his cock.

"You are just too fucking hot, Emily. I can't wait for this weekend."

"Me neither, baby," I cooed, kissing him.

Ray drove me to the train station and I picked up my car. I was only a half hour late, which was barely noticeable these days. Jenny wanted to play as soon as I was through the door and I promised her we would, but I had to help daddy make dinner. After a quick change, I found Ian in the kitchen. A large pot of pasta boiled on one side, and sauce bubbled on the other burner. I gave him a quick kiss as I fetched the garlic bread from the freezer. Davy sat at the kitchen table coloring, while Jenny played in the other room.

"Did any packages come today?" I asked.

"Actually, there was something. I put it in the office. What were you expecting?"

"It's a surprise. You can open it after dinner."

"I love surprises," Jenny shouted out of nowhere. She was suddenly behind me.

"This is a surprise for daddy. Go play until dinner is ready." I turned her around and directed her out of the kitchen.

Ian looked concerned. "Is this a good surprise, or a bad surprise?" I could see his point. There had been so much change lately that a surprise wasn't necessarily a good thing.

"It's something you didn't know you wanted. I hope you'll be pleased with it." I winked and blew him a kiss. Seeing him in this element, with the kids running around and happy I just couldn't understand what we were doing. It was so dangerous. I used to wonder why Ian would risk all this, but now I had to wonder why I did, too. After talking to Ray, I knew I wanted to fuck him just as much as Ian wanted to watch me do it. I'd had a taste, and now I wanted one night where I could just give into my urges completely and put them to bed.

"That has me intrigued. You've given me everything I wanted so far," he said meaningfully.

"My surprise will help with that." I decided this was a good a time as any to take the plunge, and lowered my voice so the kids wouldn't hear. "I talked to Ray today."

"Oh?" Ian's eyebrows went up in surprise. He was suddenly still, stopped in mid-slice, with the knife clutched in one hand and a carrot in the other.

"He's having people over to pack on Saturday. He wants me to come help." I tried to sound as casual as possible.

"Who's Ray?" Davy chimed in.

"Mommy's friend from work," Ian replied. "He's going away."

"He is? Does that make you sad, Mommy?"

I froze too, and Ian and I just stared at each other. "I'll miss him, sure. He's my friend."

"You could visit him," Davy said.

"Maybe, but he's going to be far away. I want to stay here with daddy."

"And us!"

"Of course, silly! I would never leave you guys. Even for a visit."

Ian finally went back to slicing carrots, but with a noticeably shaky hand. "So are you going over there?"

"I said I would, unless you don't want me to."

"No, you should go. I really want you to."

"Don't worry. I'll be bringing you along…sort of." And that left him confused all through dinner.

Finally, after the kids were put down, Ian and I sat on our bed and he opened the box. He looked even more confused and I couldn't help but laugh at his expression.

"It's really nice, but I don't think I have the shoes to match it," he said, holding up the Burberry knock-off purse and turning it over and around.

"No, the purse is for me to carry. Look inside it."

Ian spread the bag open and pulled out a little object that looked like a large GPS device. It was a black box with a LCD screen on one side. He still looked confused.

"Is it a videogame?"

"Give me the purse."

When he handed it over, I turned the purse around until I found the little hole for the camera. It was only slightly smaller than the end of a lipstick tube and blended perfectly with where the handle was stitched to the bag. No one would notice it, unless they were looking for it. I held it up and showed it to Ian.

"It's a hidden camera. I ordered it the other day after Ray tried to get me into his apartment the first time. It has a microphone and a wireless transmitter, so you can be in the parking lot and see what's going on. That thing is the receiver." I put the purse down and flipped through the directions.

"So I'll be able to see and hear everything that happens?" He sounded very excited. "How does it work?" He put the receiver down and picked up the purse, looking into the camera.

"It has to be charged before we can do anything. It's going to take a while, but once it's fully charged it should provided up to two hours of viewing time."

Ian cocked an eyebrow and looked at me."Is that going to be enough time?"

I knew he wanted to be playful about this, but it was difficult joking with my husband about having sex with another man. It was different when we were making love. But I gave it a shot for him.

"I don't know. Ray seems like he could go all night. I just hope I can keep up with him," I smiled.

"With you in his bed who could blame him," Ian said, reaching for me. "He probably won't want to let you go."

I brushed the purse and receiver aside and sat on his lap, where I felt his cock was already hard. I wiggled my ass and felt him surge in his shorts. "I won't know when the battery dies. Will you signal me? You can text me."

"And if you're in the middle of something?" He kneaded my breasts through my cami, rubbing my nipples with his thumbs until they were stiff and tingling. I was already turned on by going down on Ray in his car, so Ian really didn't have to do much. I raised my arms and he pulled my top off.

I pushed him back on the bed, straddling him, and pulled his t-shirt off. My hair tumbled forward as I leaned down and kissed him. He was already tugging on my loose shorts as I grinded against his hard-on. I kissed down his chest, my hair trailing behind me. When I reached the waistband of his shorts, I pulled them down. This was what I needed. I needed to be this sexy, confident woman when I was with Ray on Saturday. I had to close the door on my doubts.

"You could give us a few minutes before you warn me," I grinned evilly, and licked his cock. Ian moaned and trembled as I licked all around his head and then down the shaft.

"I...uhnnn...wouldn't want to interrupt anything, I guess..."

"You want me to have all the fun I can, don't you?" I watched him as I slipped inch after inch into my mouth and I could tell Ian wasn't focused on the blowjob, but thinking about me with Ray. He might even have been thinking about me doing this to Ray. Ian wanted to see why inner slut come out, so why was I fighting it so hard? If my husband wanted to see me like this, why should I resist? I should just enjoy myself.

"Ahhh..Em..." Ian moaned.

I gave him a last lick and then climbed on top and took him into my soaked pussy. I was so ready for him. He would probably cum in a minute if he knew why I needed him so badly. He cupped my breasts and teased my nipples while I rode him at a languid pace, enjoying the feeling of him inside me. What would it be like to have another man after so long? Making love to my husband was so wonderful, would it be the same with Ray? Or would it be hotter just because it was someone else? Or maybe I wouldn't like it at all. Somehow, I doubted that.

"Ohhh...feels *so* good...Ian..." I cooed, pouring it on. I would have never guessed how much I would like playing the sex kitten in bed.

"Em...fuck meee...ahhh...do it..."

"Let me tell you about what happened after my little talk with Ray, baby."

"Wha...what did you do?" Ian's eyes went wide and I'm sure he was thinking about the possibilities.

"After I told him I was ready to fuck him...mmm...he wanted me to go back to his place...ahhh...right then. I couldn't, not without you, baby...mmm...so I had to show him I was serious in another way...ohhhhh..."

"Em...what happened..."

I could see it in his eyes. He wanted to hear about my dirty adventure so badly. I rode him faster, grinding as I slammed down onto him. "I took out his cock and I sucked it...ahhhh...right in his front seat...it was *soo* slutty..."

"Em..."

"Come on, come on and cum...baby...I'm almost there...come on...*Ian*..."

Ian's hands shifted to my hips and he urged me faster, thrusting his hips up from the bed so that our bodies violently crashed together, sending shockwaves of pleasure through me every time I slammed down onto him. I couldn't hold out any longer and climaxed strongly. My body went rigid and I arched my back. I felt Ian expand inside me and he wailed my name as he came too. I fell forward and nuzzled him as my pussy pulsed around his prick inside me.

"So you're sure you want this?" I asked, breathlessly.

"I am. Are you really ready? If you're not…"

"I am. It's going to be a night to remember, but whatever happens at Ray's, know I love you and I'm coming home to you."

"I know. You're my wife and I love you, no matter what."

I was Ian's wife right now, but in just a couple days I would belong to another man, if only for one night. Would I be shouting as I rode Ray's cock? And would seeing me with Ray be everything Ian hoped for? I was excited for my night out now, but come Sunday morning the world could look like a very different place.

"I love you, too."

EIGHT

THE NEXT COUPLE days were a blur. All I could think about was that coming Saturday and what was going to happen. Ray, surprisingly, left me alone at work. He went from trying to get me out of my clothes at every turn to taking things completely casually. At first, I was confused, but then I thought he must be saving himself for Saturday. Either he was tired of fooling around without sex, or he thought by leaving me alone it would make me want him more. If that was true—it worked. I found Ray's sudden lack of attention frustrating. In just a few short days I'd come to rely on the heated flirting and crazy encounters we'd been having. And when I got home, I took that frustration out on my husband.

On Friday, the night before I was to go to Ray's, Ian took me from behind. As I screamed while I came, he pushed my face into the pillow. Ian had become almost unrecognizable from the man I'd married.

His obsession with watching me fuck Ray seemed to consume him in those final couple of days. He made constant references to it, G-rated when the kids were around—explicit when they weren't—and he couldn't keep his hands off me. Luckily, that coincided with my horniness. We attacked each other once the kids were in bed both nights, and the sex was incredible. While Ray had diverted some of my attention away from Ian, it was a small price to pay for our nights of passion. Leading up to the big night, we had a lot of fun testing our new hidden camera, using it to film ourselves. After all, I had to make sure I knew how to use it properly.

Saturday morning came and the last time I could remember being that nervous was when I went into labor. I knew what I was about to do was just as life-changing, but when we had the kids, Ian and I were in it together. But this was different. No matter how I looked at it, I was in this alone. Yes, Ian would be watching, but I would be the one out there, doing everything. The weight of the expectations—mine, Ian's, even Ray's, was crushing. Also, just before I gave birth, I knew it was inevitable. In a weird way, that gave me strength. Going to see Ray was still a choice, and I could still call everything off.

I considered backing out as I showered that morning, but then Ian joined me under the spray and we made love. This will sound insane, but Ian seemed to be preparing me for Ray, washing my hair and my body, even shaving me before he knelt down and kissed my smooth pussy. After I came, we made love standing up under the pelting hot water, sweet and tender. All week, we'd been fucking, but that morning—before I went off to give myself to another man—Ian and I made love.

Since other people were going to be there, and I actually had to help Ray pack, I couldn't vamp myself up too much, so I went more for everyday cute than over-the-top sexy. Layered purple and white tank tops and snug jeans covered my favorite lacy purple bra and panty set. I thought Ray would like it too, when he saw it later. Ray's friend Brian was going to be there with his girlfriend, Ashleigh. They were probably in their mid-twenties like Ray, so I hoped I fit in. I also stuffed a bikini in my special purse, since Ray said we'd probably hit the pool at some point.

When I came downstairs, Ian was in the den watching cartoons with the kids. He came out to the kitchen and we hugged each other tight. I didn't want to let him go. I was safe and secure in his arms. I could feel how much he loved me. Would he still feel the same way when I came home? Would I?

"I love you. Have fun," he said.

"I will," I replied, forcing a smile.

That was it. No last minute questions or concerns. Cooler heads did not prevail. If I hoped common sense would come riding in on a white charger and stop us, I was left waiting. Ian and I kissed and I was off.

Brian and Ashleigh were already there when I arrived at Ray's condo complex, and I could tell right away that not much packing was going to get done. They were hitting the beers early, and even though it wasn't quite eleven in the morning, I accepted one. Ray met me at the door and kissed me like we were longtime lovers. I had no idea what he'd told his friends about me, but I stiffened when his arms went around me. It wasn't quite like when we were out in public. I didn't have any practice being with Ray when other people were around. Besides, I've never been a public display of affection kind of girl, despite what I'd been doing with Ray at the bar. He wouldn't let me go until I returned the kiss, so I slithered my tongue into his mouth and pressed against him.

Ray introduced me as his friend, but I got the feeling that Brian knew there was more to our relationship than that. Suddenly, my wedding ring felt like a glowing beacon. I just told myself I would never see this people again and plowed on. And the beer helped. I drained the first quickly and Ashleigh fetched me another.

The music was cranked up and we got into a groove. Collapsed boxes were stacked in the corner and Ashleigh and I went to work on packing up the kitchen while the boys disassembled the entertainment center. She was a cute girl—just Ray's type, I thought. Blonde hair halfway down her back and big blue eyes made her the perfect all-American girl, and she had the curves of a beauty queen. Ashleigh looked like she was barely out of college, making me really feel my age. Luckily, she was quite chatty and did not ask too many questions, so I could just listen and not make up any stories about my own life.

The boys checked on us from time to time, and came into the kitchen for fresh beers. Brian and Ashleigh were quite affectionate with each other, which helped me relax and more receptive to Ray's overtures. When he nuzzled me from behind, I leaned into him and turned to kiss him on the cheek, though I did stop his hand before it reached my breast. I wasn't about to let him grope me in front of his friends.

We ordered in for pizza around one, and sat in the cluttered living room eating, using boxes as tables and making the best of the limited space. I was glad for the food because the beers were really going to my head. Ray and I sat cross-legged on the floor, while Ashleigh sat in Brian's lap. By the time we finished lunch, no one was in the mood to work and Ray suggested we hit the pool for a while. Brian went into the guest room to change, while Ashleigh pulled off her tight t-shirt right there.

Her bikini—what there was of it—was right under her outfit. The cups of her multi-colored bikini top strained to contain her, and the strings looked ready to give up the fight at any second. My catty side emerged, and I wondered if I'd get any attention at all in my more modest two-piece. I went into Ray's room to change and he followed me.

"Let me help you with that," he said, pulling at my layered tank tops from behind. I raised my arms over my head and let him strip me. His expression when I turned and showed off the purple demi-cups that offered up my breasts made me smile. I didn't have to worry about Ashleigh stealing my thunder.

I stepped forward and he covered my breasts with his hands. Thumbs flicked my exposed nipples, bringing them instantly hard, and I cooed as I pushed into his hands. I grabbed him around the neck and pulled him into a hot kiss while he unhooked my bra in the back. His lips were sucking a nipple before my bra hit the floor and I threw my head back with a quiet moan. We went from zero to sixty in seconds, and I had to push him away before we ended up on the queen-sized bed, among scattered shirts and jeans.

"You're not here just to tease me again are you?" Ray said with a grin, grabbing at me as I spun away.

"No, but we're not going to screw with your friends in the next room. What do they know about me anyway?" I put my purse on the bed and wiggled out of my jeans.

"Just that you're a friend from work." He pulled off his clinging t-shirt, exposing that hard chest of his, and I swear my pussy tightened just a little. I could never get tired of seeing that man naked.

"Nothing more?"

"No, nothing more. But they might figure it out if we keep acting the way we have been." He dropped his pants and boxer briefs, standing with his semi-hard cock sticking out. It was hard to look away. All I could think about was how he was going to feel inside me. Ray was quite thick and I was sure he knew how to use what he had.

"Then maybe we should cool it," I said, but that wasn't what I wanted. *You're the sexy and confident one today*, I told myself. *Who cares what the others see?*

Wearing only panties, I walked over and wrapped my hand around him. His shaft was hot to the touch and grew even larger in my hand. I also played with his balls, then quickly knelt down and licked the precum that formed on the head of his prick. I smiled, then turned and walked away to change. Now that was the woman I needed to be!

"How am I supposed to go out there like this?" Ray complained.

"Throw some cold water on it," I laughed.

While I was changing into my eggplant-colored two-piece, with big white polka dots, I looked around the bedroom for a good perch to place the camera later. I couldn't put it someplace odd, but much of the bedroom was already packed, so there were boxes conveniently stacked by the foot of the bed. The black lacquered headboard had a shelf with an alarm clock and a paperback, and I thought it would make a good vantage point for Ian. I wondered if it would be weird for me without knowing he was there, physically. At least I was able to see him on a monitor before things started with Ray in the tele-conference room. Here, I would just have to trust he was out there, watching me. If I was honest with myself, I would have realized it was becoming far too easy to be intimate with Ray whether my husband was there to watch me or not. He didn't witness those times I blew Ray in his car. Ian wasn't here when I'd just teased Ray a moment ago. But I wanted to be able to tell myself that I was mostly doing this for Ian, so I ignored all that.

I stole into the bathroom and texted Ian to let him know I was headed to the pool, and that I would be testing the camera. I didn't want to leave it on too long because I had to save the battery for the main event. I didn't know if my husband was connected yet. He should have taken the kids to his parents by now, so he should be ready. I couldn't see much of the parking lot when we walked out to the pool. There were maybe a dozen or so other people around, but we were able to stake out an area for ourselves.

Ashleigh wiggled out of her short, tight cut-offs at the pool, revealing a butt just as round as her breasts. I thought she was definitely the type Ray usually bedded. I put my purse at the foot of a lounge and surreptitiously activated the camera when I look my suntan lotion out of it. The camera was angled toward me and I tried to put on a good show for Ian as I rubbed the lotion into my pale, freckled skin. I burn easily and the last thing I needed was a sunburn to ruin the evening. Once I was properly protected, I put the purse on the ground between my lounge and Ashleigh's, with the camera pointed toward the pool. I walked over and sat by the edge, where Ray and Brian were talking. I dangled my legs in the water and Brian went back over to Ashleigh.

Then, after a few moments, Brian and Ashleigh rejoined us. Suddenly, on a signal I must have missed, the boys lifted me and tossed me into the water. Ashleigh followed, nearly losing her bikini top. We received a disapproving look from the lifeguard, a petite teenager with sun-whitened blonde hair and deep tan. *Was that the girl who told Ray how to get into the pool after hours?* I wondered jealously. As we didn't have the pool to ourselves, we were forced to behave, but it was fun to goof around in the water with the others and not think about anything else but being in the moment. I didn't mind when Ray groped me beneath the water, and may have done some groping in return, but we really did behave. If anything, Brian and Ashleigh put us to shame. They, apparently, had no problem with public displays. For a second I thought someone was going to have to intervene before they just did it right there in front of everyone.

We returned to our loungers to dry off and I reached down to kill the camera. I'd already left it on longer than I'd planned. There couldn't have been much for Ian to see while we were in the pool. We all lay in the hot sun and I think I may have drifted off for a couple minutes while the others talked about old times. I don't know how much time had passed, but I heard Brian say they were going to head inside, change to go back to the hotel where they were staying. They were planning to hit a club they'd heard about, and asked if we wanted to join them, but Ray said we had other plans.

"So do you really have plans?" I asked, once the others were gone.

"You have no idea. I hope you've been taking your vitamins. You're going to need your energy," Ray chuckled.

"I might surprise you. I can handle a young buck like you," I teased, feeling silly even as I said it.

"Oh, I bet you'll surprise me."

After another half hour, we headed back to Ray's apartment, figuring the coast was clear. I was planning to shower and do something with my make-up, but as soon as we walked in, we heard that Brian and Ashleigh were still there. Ray motioned for me to be quiet and softly closed the door. It seemed that the other couple hadn't heard us come in.

The sounds coming from the guest bedroom were unmistakable and I looked at Ray curiously. *What was he up to?* I thought that we should either announce our presence, or leave. Instead, Ray was nudging me forward, closer to the bedroom. I was not about to look in on the other couple having sex, even if I was interested. Just hearing them going at it was hot, and I could feel my body reacting.

Ashleigh's high-pitched moans were almost comical and it was hard to tell if they were from pleasure or pain. Only her occasional urgent murmurs of "Baby, baby" gave the clue. Brian was grunting with great effort and the sounds of flesh slapping together filled the apartment. I would have enjoyed seeing him in action. Brian was just as fit as Ray, but his hair was cropped down to the scalp and he had a goatee that gave him an edgier look. He was like the bad boy version of Ray. The longer we stood there and listened, the more I realized I did want to peek. I finally understood some of what Ian must feel when he watches me, although I was sure that seeing him with another woman—something I had no desire to do—would be much different than spying on Ray's hot friend.

Ray was behind me and he swept my wet hair away so he could nibble on the side of my neck. I leaned back, and his bulge pushed into the small of my back. He worked his hand inside my swimsuit top and fingered my sensitive nipple. Though I bit my lip and suppressed my moan, it became more of a struggle when he slipped a hand into my bikini bottom and touched my pussy. I was already damp, and his fingers got me wet in a hurry. He stroked my clit and I bit my fist to stifle moans. I rubbed back against Ray's cock, wanting to tease him too. If only the camera had been on for this! I knew Ian would have loved it.

I did not resist when Ray moved us forward again. He bent me so I could see around the door frame, and there they were. Ashleigh sat on a dresser, with her face buried in Brian's chest, her legs wrapped around him, while he stood and pumped away at her. I don't really enjoy watching porn, but seeing two people having sex in the flesh was intoxicating. Ray rubbed my clit harder and my legs felt rubbery. I was scared that if I came, I couldn't be quiet and we'd be found out, but I couldn't help myself.

Ray pulled me back and into the kitchen. He pushed me against the refrigerator and jammed his hand back into my bottom, pushing it down. Two fingers slipped inside me and the knuckle on his thumb mashed my clit. He kissed me hard, cutting off my moan and fingered me rapidly. I reached into his trunks and grabbed his stiff meat, but I climaxed before I could do anything but squeeze it. My muffled cries poured into Ray's mouth and at the same time Ashleigh released a high-pitched squeal, like someone was letting all of her air out. Ray let me go and I started slipping to the floor before I caught myself. He moved to the door, opened it and then slammed it loudly.

"You guys still here?" he announced.

"Uh, yeah, we'll be right out," Brian stammered.

I fixed my swimsuit and hurried over to Ray, who'd just walked into the living room. Moments later, Brian and Ashleigh emerged from the guestroom. Their clothes looked hastily arranged. I barely suppressed my smile.

"Sorry, we must have lost track of time," Ashleigh apologized, her face three shades of red. I don't know if it was from embarrassment or exertion.

"Hey, *mi casa es su casa*, at least as long as it's still *mi casa*," Ray chuckled.

I found myself looking at the younger couple enviously. Seeing the way Brian took Ashleigh made me want him for myself. I knew I was going to have fun with Ray, but my wicked side wondered why I couldn't have both. *Those dark fantasies really are bubbling up*, I thought.

"We'd better get going," Ashleigh said, pulling Brian toward the door.

"Are you sure you don't want to come along with us tonight?" Brian asked.

"Yeah, but thanks anyway," Ray replied.

"It was nice meeting you, Emily," Ashleigh called out from the door.

"Likewise," I said. And then they were gone.

The second the door closed, Ray and I were all over each other. I pulled at his shirt while he fumbled with untying my top at the back of my neck. I won the race and pulled his shirt over his head. I was kissing that sexy, muscular chest when he succeeded untying my top. He just let it drop down and mashed my breasts in both hands. I gasped when he pinched both nipples between his fingers at the same time. He was maneuvering me back toward the couch when I snatched my last strands of self-control and pushed him away.

"What?" Ray said with exasperation.

"We are not having a quickie on the couch. We're going to do this right. I'm going into the bedroom to get ready and then I will call you in," I patted his chest like I was calming an angry animal.

"You're killing me, Em."

I kissed him and smiled. "I promise, it will all be worth it."

With a quick wave, I closed the bedroom door and peeled out of my swimsuit. The first thing I wanted to do was take a shower and call Ian. I took my phone into the bathroom and dialed him as I started the water.

"Hey, what's going on?" He picked up on the first ring.

"We're just about ready. Are you?" I tried to keep my voice down, but wanted him to hear me over the running water. I twisted the knobs to get the hot-cold mixture right.

"I have been. Who was that blonde by the pool?" I could hear the eagerness in his voice.

"That was Ashleigh, his friend's girlfriend. Don't get too excited, dear. They left, so there will be no threesome."

"A guy can dream, can't he?"

"Anyway, I have to go. I just wanted to make sure you're ready. I'm going to rinse the chlorine off, then it's show time."

"Great."

"You still want this?" I bit my lip. I didn't know what I would have done if he said no.

"I do."

"Okay. Gotta go." I hung up, put the phone on the counter and jumped into the stream of steaming water. As I smoothed my hair back, I thought, *Here we go!*

After my hair was washed and my body scrubbed clean, I found Ray's hairdryer. I just knew a man like him would have one. I simply dried my hair and brushed it so it hung straight back. Simplest was best, I thought. I dabbed on some perfume and fixed my make-up, dark kohl around my eyes and the same slutty red lipstick I'd worn the other night. I took a condom from my purse and placed it on the shelf where it would be within easy reach. I put my lingerie set back on and finally, I activated the camera. I arranged the bag until I knew it was pointed down at the bed. I'm sure both my men—Ray in the next room, and my husband outside—were impatient, but I wanted everything to be perfect. I called out to Ray to let him know I was ready.

Ray walked into the bedroom wearing nothing but a cocky smile. I couldn't help staring at him. From those broad shoulders to his muscular thighs, and especially what hung between them, he was like perfection. I couldn't believe this sexy man wanted me. I walked around the bed, careful not to block the camera, and rubbed against his body while we kissed, but only for a moment. Ray grinned when I took his hand and led him to the bed. He lay in the middle and I crawled on the dark red sheets between his legs.

"Why aren't I surprised you that like to take the lead in bed?" he chuckled.

"I just want to show you just how much I want you, and how sorry I am for keeping you waiting. Tonight, I'm yours, baby. You can have me however you want me."

Pushing my hair back over my shoulders, I leaned forward and took him in my mouth once again. I've always liked giving oral, but I had never been into it so much as with Ray. His cock seemed perfect, thick and hard and beautiful, and all I wanted to do was pleasure it. Every time we were together, I couldn't help myself and I had to blow him. I held him with both hands and lovingly licked his shaft from base to tip, sucking and tonguing the head until Ray was shaking and gasping my name. I licked back down the underside, then sucked on those big balls. My eyes shifted from my lover's to the camera poised above the bed. I imagined I was looking right at my husband as I sucked on Ray's balls. Was I giving him what he wanted? Did he want to see me give myself to another man so completely? My lips smacked when I released Ray's balls, then his cock was in my mouth again and I was sucking him hard. I bobbed quickly, with my cheeks hollowed, and Ray kept my hair pulled back from my face. I loved the way he looked at me when I sucked his cock.

"Fuck...Em...fuck that's good...so fucking good..." Ray moaned, lifting his hips from the bed. I let him pump his cock into my mouth, but used my hand around the base to keep him from choking me. I thought he might stop me so we could finally have sex, but instead he held onto my head and a couple seconds later he was shooting his creamy load into my mouth. I greedily swallowed every drop and kept sucking him. His shaft never went totally flaccid.

"I love making you cum," I told him, crawling up to cover his body with mine.

"And you do it so well. I should return the favor."

We kissed and he rolled us over, so that I was on my back. His deep crimson sheets were so soft against my skin, it felt like I was floating on a cloud. I closed my eyes as he kissed my neck and pulled my bra straps from my shoulders.

"You look good in purple, but I bet you'll look even better out of it," he joked, kissing my breast through my bra.

"Ray," I moaned softly when his teeth nipped at my swelling nipple through the thin, rough lace. "Ohh, baby…"

He moved from side to side, kissing and biting at both my nipples without taking off my bra. It was such a delicious tease. I yearned to feel his lips on my naked flesh and tried to pull my bra out of the way, but he stopped me and bit one of my throbbing nipples even harder. I was right on the edge of pleasure and pain and I cried out.

"*Please…*"

"You love to tease me so much, I think I should return the favor," he laughed.

"God, don't stop, Ray…"

He peeled my bra back and sucked hard on a nipple, attacking it with his tongue. I cried out and arched my back, shoving my flesh into his mouth. He held my slender body with an arm around my back and also slipped a hand between my legs. I was soaked already, and my panties clung to my smooth mound. When he squeezed my pussy, I cried out even louder and dug my nails into his shoulders. He easily flicked my bra clasp open and threw it away. Ray pressed me back onto the bed and forced my arms over my head, holding both wrists in one, strong hand. He was free to ravage my breasts and I was powerless to stop him. I twisted and whimpered and moaned his name. Just kissing and sucking my breasts, he had me on the edge of climax and begging for more.

"Please…please…take me…Ray…" I cried. I wanted him to fuck me so badly. I was so ready, but he made me wait.

Ray pulled my panties off and pushed my legs apart. I tried to pull him up on top of me again, but he resisted and instead kissed my pussy. I think I literally screamed when he sucked on my clit. I grabbed the pillow and mashed it in my hands while humping my pussy at Ray. He was merciless with his tongue and he made me cum so fast I thought I was losing my mind.

"Ray...*God!*" I cried, my pussy gushing while he licked and slurped between my legs. His tongue brought me right to the edge of a second orgasm before he stopped.

"I guess you've waited long enough," he said, moving over me and kissing me.

"I want you, baby. I want you so much," I cooed, kissing him frantically.

"Tell me what you want, Em. Say it."

"I want you to fuck me. I want your cock," I breathed. I couldn't believe the words came so easily. *Ian must be eating this up*, I thought. I knew Ian had to be rock hard and I thought he might even be touching himself. God, I wished I could see that too. The camera was good, but I wished my husband was there with us. I so wanted to be able to see him watching me. Maybe he would even join in. Having two men was one of my darker fantasies, but I was ready to do it in that moment. I wished I could suck Ian while Ray took my pussy.

"Then take it. Put it inside you, baby," Ray demanded.

I loved feeling his power and strength and reached for him. There was only one thing to do before I finally enjoyed him. I tore the wrapper open with my teeth and then slipped it over his shaft. Ray never questioned my wanting the condom, which pleased me. *Now* we were ready. His cock was hot and just as hard as ever. His fat head split my lips and I whimpered. He pushed my hand away and buried himself in me with one swift thrust. I bit my lip and my eyes went wide. He felt even better inside me than I'd imagined. He felt bigger. He filled me and kept it in my pulsing pussy while I squirmed underneath him and made little moaning sounds. Ray pinned my arms over my head again and began thrusting. He was slow, pulling almost completely out before ramming it back in and jolting my entire body. His eyes kept locked to mine.

"I've wanted to fuck you for so long, Em," he grunted. "I've thought about this so many times."

"Uhhnn...Ray..."

"The way you teased around the office, I knew you were fucking hot for it. I knew you needed more than you were getting."

"*Ray*..." I didn't like what he was saying, but the power in his words inflamed me. I didn't want him putting Ian down, not when he was listening, but all I could do was moan while my younger lover took me.

"And then you started fucking teasing me...you wouldn't give it up, but I knew you wanted it...fuck you feel good..."

"Yesss...yessss...Raayyyy..."

"God, you're a fucking great cocksucker, but I had to fuck you, Em."

"Fuck me! *Fuck me*...Raayyyy..."

His slow, methodical approach was almost more than I could bear, so I was happy when he started pounding me. He drove that hard cock down into me like he was trying to ram me through the bed. God that was what I needed. I needed him to take me hard. I wanted to be fucked like the slut I was. I wanted my husband to see me used. I hoped he was enjoying the show as much as I was. I wrapped my legs around Ray, pulling him into me.

"So fucking good...you're so fucking hot..." Ray grunted.

"Fuck me! *Fuck me*!" I begged over and over.

I cried out that I was cumming and Ray pulled out. I suddenly felt empty and reached for him. He roughly flipped me over and pulled my butt into the air. He rammed back into me while I was still cumming and he could barely get into my tightened pussy.

"What a fucking ass!" Ray exclaimed. He held my hips and plowed me from behind. I clawed at the sheets and shamelessly begged him to fuck me. It felt like I would never stop cumming. He jackhammered me with my face buried in the sheets and even smacked my ass. I didn't care. I wanted whatever he had to give. I don't know how long we fucked like that, but he pulled out once again, and I collapsed to the bed.

Ray held me and kissed me and I wrapped my hand around his cock, almost wishing the condom wasn't there. The man was a stallion. It was like he could stay hard all night. A girl could have fun with a man like that. He massaged my breasts and played with my pussy, working two fingers inside me while I steadily fucked them. When fooling around wasn't enough anymore, I slid on top and mounted him.

"Ah, yeah, fuck me, Em. Ride it," Ray moaned, sliding his hands from my hips up to my breasts. He pulled and teased my nipples, and I squeezed his cock inside me.

"Ohhh...baby...I love your cock...I love fucking you...Rayyy..." By that point I wasn't sure if I was performing for Ian any longer—or just saying what I felt.

"I'm gonna fuck you all night."

"Yesss...yesss..."

I didn't stare at Ray this time. I was staring right into the camera. Right at my husband. *I'm fucking him*, I thought, like Ian could hear me. *I'm fucking Ray, just like you wanted. It's so fucking good, honey. He's fucking me so good. Do you like it? Do you like me being your little slut?* God, I wished he was there. I wanted to tell him those things. *Ray's making me cum so hard, honey. I can't help myself. I love it!*

While I was focused on my husband, Ray was finally ready to finish and his grip tightened on my hips. He took over, guiding my movements and effortless lifted me up and down, pistoning his cock like I was his sex toy. I swear I felt him swelling inside me just before he came.

"*Emily…*" Ray cried.

Ray jammed me down, and as I was grinding my pelvis into his, all his pent up desire released itself and he came deep inside me. Even though he'd already cum in my mouth, it still felt like my younger lover was cumming forever. I came again just after he did, gripping the headboard and leaning forward so my face was right in the camera. It wasn't quite the simultaneous orgasms Ian and I occasionally enjoy, but it was close and it was wonderful. So what did Ian think, as he watched me cumming, almost simultaneously, with another man?

When we finished, I snuggled close into Ray's side and enjoyed touching his hard, toned body. I won't lie. I was going to miss having him to play with. His spent cock twitched when I touched it, reminding me of how much stamina a young, fit man has.

"Baby, that was so good," I cooed, kissing his chest. His fingers tossed my wild, chestnut hair and he kissed my forehead.

"You were fucking incredible, Em. It was even better than I thought it would be. Holy shit, babe. You're like a fucking machine."

"Really?" I am sure I blushed.

"That's what's so hot about older women."

"Watch it," I said, playfully hitting his chest.

"No, it's good. You know your body, you know what you want. And when a chick keeps herself in shape like you do, damn, it's a knockout combination."

"So you aren't jealous of your friend Brian, that he has someone like Ashleigh?"

"You kidding? A girl like that can't hold a candle to a woman like you in bed. He's probably jealous of me."

"Now you're just being crazy."

I moved to get out of bed, but Ray pulled me back down, and we kissed when I landed on top of him. I felt him growing between my thighs once more while our tongues dashed against each other.

"You don't think we're done yet, do you?" Ray asked, grabbing my butt.

I didn't know what I should do, since Ian had doggedly refused to discuss anything in detail. Was I supposed to just fuck Ray and hightail it out of there? I knew what I wanted, and I was not ready to leave yet. If this was my one night of freedom, I decided to indulge it completely.

"No, but I would like to get some water," I said. "Would you like something?"

"I have everything I want right here."

"Goofball. I'll be right back." I rolled off of him, then the bed, and found one of Ray's discarded work shirts. I just buttoned two of the middle buttons as I walked out of the bedroom.

I was startled by Brian, who seemed to appear from nowhere. The apartment was dark, so all my attention was focused on not walking into any boxes, and I didn't see him until I almost walked into him in the kitchen. I uttered a short cry and would have fallen if he hadn't caught me.

"Is everything okay?" Ray called from the bedroom.

Brian shushed me, and I was so startled that I obeyed.

"Uh, yeah. I just walked into something."

Although I enjoyed being up against Brian while I was half-naked, I pushed back and whispered, "What are you doing here?"

"Ashleigh forgot her phone, so I told her I'd swing back to get it while got ready for the nightclub.. It takes her forever to get ready," he said, never once making eye contact.

"Don't dare make some crack about how all women take forever to get ready," As my eyes finally adjusted and I could make out his face, I suddenly realized just how exposed I was. The shirt I had grabbed gaped open at the cleavage and between the shirttails. If it hadn't been so dark in the kitchen he would have seen everything.

"You look ready right now," he grinned. It was a goofy, open smile, which contrasted with Ray's sly, seductive grin. While they were both big, buff guys, there was a contrast. Ray was dark and dangerous, Brian was blond and seemed fun, like a surfer boy.

"Ready for what?" I asked, regretting the words as soon as they came out of my mouth. How long had he been listening to us?

Brian pulled me close by the front of the shirt and we kissed. When I tried to push away, he held my head and his arm went around my back, trapping me, not that I struggled for very long. Soon my fingers were mussing his shaggy, sandy hair and my tongue was in his mouth, while his hand dropped to my butt and massaged it. He easily lifted me and sat me on the counter, going for the buttons on the front of my shirt.

"Ray is just in the next room," I weakly protested. I wasn't really asking him to stop. Now that I was over the line, I didn't care what happened anymore, I just wanted to fool around. But if we were going to do this, I wanted it to be in front of the camera.

"He won't mind. Back when we were roommates in college, we shared everything," he replied, nipping at my neck.

As Brian pushed my shirt open, I realized that my fantasy of having two men was going to come true. I would leave no stone unturned tonight. His hands went to my breasts and my full, throbbing nipples pressed into his palms. I pulled him into another kiss when he teased my nipples, if only to stifle my moans. Yes, this was going to happen, but my husband was not going to be one of the men! What would Ian think when another man came back into the bedroom with me? Hadn't I told him Brian was gone? Would my husband think I was a liar? Fear stabbed my heart as I thought that this could be a step too far. It could ruin everything. Ian might not be prepared for this, but I truly could not control myself.

"Ray's going to wonder where I am, baby," I moaned when Brian kissed and licked one of my nipples. He rubbed my swollen, red mound and I leaned my head back against the cabinets, wiggling my butt on the cold countertop.

"Then let's go see him," he chuckled.

Brian seemed to think nothing of taking me in his arms and carrying me back into the bedroom. Ray looked surprised, but not angry, making me wonder if this was some kind of set-up. I don't think most men would be too happy if another man, even a friend, brought their lover back to the bedroom.

"I was wondering where you were. Guess you ran into some*one* rather than some*thing*," Ray said.

"He was just out there, I didn't..." I said, just as much for Ian as for Ray. I didn't want either of them angry with me.

"It's cool. As long as I get you to myself most of the night, I don't mind sharing with an old friend for a while. I told you he wanted you too," Ray laughed.

"He's right, I was checking you out all day. Ray's got great taste in women," Brian said. He put me on my feet and pulled the shirt off from behind me.

"You boys are talking like I have no say in this." My words trailed off into a sigh when Brian swept my hair aside and started kissing my neck from behind. His other hand went around me and stroked my pussy. A finger pushed between my lips and dipped inside me. I moaned loudly and raised up on the balls of my feet. God, I was sensitive down there. I could only imagine what Ian was seeing as I stood at the foot of the bed with Brian ravishing me from behind.

Ray crawled over and knelt at the foot of the bed and kissed my breasts. I twisted my head and kissed Brian while Ray nibbled on my nipples. Brian found my clit and I drowned in the sensations. It was like I was in the sexiest dream ever when they maneuvered me onto the bed. I was on my side between them, kissing Ray while they both touched me everywhere. Brian kissed my neck and shoulder. I turned onto my back and took turns kissing each of them, then I reached down and stroked both their cocks. I don't even know when Brian lost his clothes. Brian was not quite as large as his friend, but there was more than enough there to fulfill my needs.

I purred like a contented cat when the boys simultaneously kissed my breasts, and I moaned loudly when they sucked and licked my nipples. It was heavenly! I held both of their heads to my chest and whispered encouragement. They pulled my legs wider apart and, by the way one rubbed my clit while the other fingered me, I could tell these guys had some practice at this. Under their expert attentions, I came quickly, crying out in pleasure as I bucked against their hands. I was so insanely wet that I'm sure I left a big damp spot beneath where they played with my pussy. Ray brought his drenched fingers to my lips and I greedily sucked them clean.

The boys did not want to let me up, but I untangled from their hands and turned to kneel on the bed between them. I smiled and said, "What am I going to do with these two strong, young cocks?" They both chuckled as I pushed my hair back and leaned forward. I sucked Ray first, since I was his woman for the night. I stared up at him as his prick disappeared into my mouth.

"Wait 'til you get a load of this," Ray said to Brian, then moaned, holding my hair back from my face as I bobbed up and down with hollowed cheeks. I let him go with a quick lick of his swollen red head, then turned my attention to Brian.

"Goddamn," Brian exclaimed when I licked his shaft up and down. My hair fell in my face again and I wished I had something to hold it back, but then Brian obliged and held it back with both hands, watching as I licked back to the head and then sucked on it. His eyes widened as I took inch after inch into my mouth. I couldn't swallow the whole thing, but I stroked when I couldn't wrap my lips around it and I sucked hard on what I had. I looked up past him and into the camera, imagining I was looking my husband in the eye as I sucked on this fresh cock.

With his fingers in my hair, Brian started guiding me up and down, making me sucking him faster. I let him have control for a couple minutes, but then I returned to Ray's cock. I went like that for a while, sucking one and then the other, making them wait for it. But in the end, I was the one who couldn't wait any longer. My pussy was on fire. I needed one of these guys inside me right away.

"How are we going to do this, guys?" I asked.

"Someone can't wait to get fucked," Ray chuckled.

"You're right. Less talking, more screwing," I replied. With those two hard cocks staring up at me, I felt at the height of my sexual powers.

"I hate to leave a pretty lady waiting," Brian said.

Brian reached out and pulled me on top of him. I had no idea how something like this was supposed to work, but it appeared they planned to take turns. Ray tossed Brian a condom—I guess Ray really had been prepared—and both boys sheathed up. The blond hunk held his cock and fit it inside me. I sank onto him with a long, low moan. God, I felt so filled when I took him to the hilt. Brian roughly massaged my breasts, and I put my hands on his muscular chest as I worked my hips and started riding him. I was embarrassed by the my way ripe pussy squished around his shaft, but it didn't stop me from riding him faster and faster.

"Ohhh…it feels sooo good…" I gasped. I loved the way he stretched me open when I bottomed out on him. He was so thick at the base.

"Goddamn, your pussy is fucking tight." Brian moaned, sliding his hands from my chest to my ass. He kneaded my cheeks roughly, then pulling me into him so we ground together every time I dropped onto him.

"Ohhh…ohhh…fuck me…fuck me!" I cried. I looked over at Ray, who seemed content to lay on his side and watch us while stroking his cock. Now I was being watched by two men while I fucked some young stud I barely knew. It all made me so hot. My audience was growing! Maybe I was on the road to being a porn star! All I knew was that I loved being watched.

"You're a fucking little slut, aren't you?" Brian grunted.

"Yesss…yesss…I'm a fucking slut for you guys…"

I screamed in aggravation when Ray pulled me off of his friend. I was getting close to cumming, and I needed it so badly. He rolled me onto my back and knelt between my legs. Holding my hips, he lifted me to him and I reached for his prick. My head and shoulders rested on the bed while a kneeling Ray pulled me up and onto his cock. He was so strong, he easily handed my body, and I loved this new position. He slammed me back and forth onto his shaft and I grabbed onto my bouncing breasts while I cried out.

Brian didn't want to wait on the sidelines like Ray. He knelt beside my head and turned my face so his rock hard cock was right in my face. His condom was gone. The head pressed against my lips and I opened wide, tasting the latex that had just covered him. In that prone position, I really had no control, and that was the beginning of the guys using my body. Brian fed me his cock and Ray slammed me onto his at the other end. Brian held the back of my head as he fucked my mouth and I was filled by both men. Honestly, this was what I pictured in my dark fantasies. It wasn't guys taking turns, it was two men using me at the same time. And that was exactly what my young lovers did.

I don't know how long they fucked me in that position, but I did scream into Brian's cock as Ray made me climax. Ray pulled his dripping cock from me and I was turned around – not sure by who – onto my hands and knees. Brian took me from behind while Ray took my mouth. All of my hair was gathered in Ray's fist, and he used it to pull me forward until his cock was choking me. Then Brian, with hands on my hips, pulled me back so I was impaled on his prick. One cock entered me and the other slipped away and it felt like one long cock driving through me, like I was on a spit over a fire. It was so slutty, so dirty. It was amazing! I could barely keep track of what was going on, and I was passively waiting to find out what they wanted next when the boys both pulled out of me again.

Ray put me on my side, with one leg in the air and knelt between my legs. He slammed right into me again, and I hungrily sucked Brian's cock when he gave it to me. He let me lick it, but it was hard to concentrate much on him with Ray fucking me at the other end. How many times had I cum by then? Two, three times? Brian seemed to be teasing me, rubbing his cock across my face as I stared up at him.

"You want my cock?" Brian asked.

"Yess..ohhhh…yesss…please…" I begged. I tried to get him in my mouth, but he still teased me.

"Say it again."

"Please give it to me…give me your cock…ohhhhhh… Rayyyyyy…" I was screaming his friend's name when Brian shoved his cock back into my mouth. God, I was their whore! I'd turned into a whore and it was my husband that pushed me to do it. Shouldn't I have been angry? I couldn't worry about that because, incredibly, I was cumming again.

I was turned one more time. While I was face down on the bed, Brian took me from behind. Ray sat with his back against the headboard and held my head while his cock filled my mouth. He just let the force of Brian's fucking drive me forward onto him. Brian reached under me, and when he rubbed my clit, my screams were muted only because my mouth was stuffed full of Ray. Otherwise, neighbors would be calling the police. Brian took his wet finger and started playing with my ass. I squirmed, but there was no way for me to get away, and after some teasing, which filled me with a new, strange tingling, he started to push.

My ass has always been a no-fly zone in my marriage. None of my earlier boyfriends ever really made a serious attempt to take me back there, but Ian had expressed some interest. When he brought it up, I shut him down cold. I wouldn't even let him play with a finger back there. Honestly, it just scared me. I had heard that any kind of anal was painful, and I just wasn't interested in that. But here I was, and I didn't have any choice but to let Brian play. His slick index finger pushed past my resistance and I screamed into Ray's cock. Brian slowly fingered my ass, which seemed to turn him on even more, because he started fucking me even faster. For the first time in my life, I had every entrance filled.

Ray felt me shaking and took his cock out of my mouth. I felt like my eyes were going to roll up into my head. His wet cock slapped against my cheek as Brian fucked and fingered me at the other end.

"Uhnn...yes...uhnn...fuck...fuck...uhnnn...ohhhhhh... God...yessss..." I cried. I had never felt anything like that. It was like I'd left my own body and some kind of demon had possessed it.

A demon who loved to fuck. I didn't even recognize my voice as I screamed and begged to cum. I felt Brian cumming inside me and that was the trigger. I came too, howling holy terror, and Brian kept fucking me until he was drained and limp and couldn't go any longer.

Once Brian was done with me, Ray rolled me onto my back and put my legs up over his shoulders and finished with me, slamming so hard that his balls were bouncing off of me. I don't think I was capable of cumming again, but I was happy to please him, and loved it when I felt him cumming. I was left to lay, as though boneless, on the bed, while the guys stood beside it talking.

"Hey, thanks for sharing man. Emily's a fucking incredible piece of ass," Brian said as he pulled his pants on.

"No problem. Just be prepared to party with Ashleigh when I get back to Philly," Ray replied.

"Sure. How long have you been tapping that?"

"Believe it or not, this is the first night. We've been fooling around, but I never banged her before."

Brian laughed. "Guess she was saving the best for last. Dude, I need to bolt. Ashleigh is going to wonder where I've been."

"No worries, man."

"Goodnight sweetheart. Be good," Brian said to me. He leaned over and kissed my cheek, then he was gone.

I was lying across the width of the bed, with my legs hanging off, so Ray turned me, then lay down beside me. He pulled me close and kissed me. Exhausted, I snuggled into him.

"You are fucking unbelievable. How the fuck have you been hiding all that, all this time? Holy shit, you're a fucking wet dream, Em."

His words made me glow, even though he was essentially telling me what an incredible slut I was. It was what I wanted to hear. It meant that I'd lived up to – or down to – everyone's expectations. The night had exceeded my wildest dreams and as Ray went on about my sexual prowess, I drifted off to sleep.

NINE

EVERYTHING ACHED WHEN I rolled over to see what time it was. Panic filled my heart when the bedside clock wasn't there, and I realized the dark bedroom wasn't mine. That meant Ian wasn't the man in bed with me. Before I completely freaked out, everything came rushing back, and a little smile came to my lips. Oh yes, that wasn't my husband in bed beside me. I was a very bad wife. And as the night's events came back to me, I realized that things had gotten a little *too crazy*. I was adamant that I wanted to use condoms with Ray when we finally had sex, but I hadn't planned on Brian being there—things got wild quickly and as the boys shoved their cocks into my mouth they shed their condoms and I just went with it. I didn't even think about it at the time. I was just focused on pleasing the boys and how many times they were making me climax. I wasn't too worried about pregnancy, but I would have to make sure to get tested for everything else.

Ray was in a very deep sleep, so I eased out of bed as best as I could, and gathered what clothes I could find in the dark, before I tip-toed into the bathroom and turned on the light. Oh my God, I was a mess! My thick auburn hair was tangled and seemed to go in all directions. Lipstick was smeared all over my face, and there were red marks all over my body where I'd been manhandled. I was red and swollen down below, and sore to the touch. My muscles ached all over and all together I looked and felt like I'd been run over by a truck.

It was like a slut hangover.

A hot shower alleviated some of the aches and pains, and it felt good to scrub my body clean. I vigorously washed my hair, but gingerly washed my pussy. I knew Ian was going to want to make love when I got home, but it was going to be tough.

Oh God, Ian. When I got out of the shower I checked my phone. It was after three in morning and there were no messages from my husband. I was not supposed to spend the night with Ray. I could only guess that Ian was angry I hadn't come home yet. I knew I should call him, but I chickened out and put my phone away.

After dressing in just my jeans and one tank top, I couldn't find the rest of my clothes in the dark, I slipped out of the bathroom and tried to find the rest of my things by the light of my cell phone. I was hoping to sneak out without waking Ray.

"You were just going to leave?" Ray asked in the dark. I saw him sit up in bed, the sheet falling to his lap.

"I didn't want to wake you. I have to get home. Ian is going to kill me." Since the cat was out of the bag, I turned on the light. He watched as I gathered my things.

"If you're already in trouble, you might as well stay."

I laughed. "That's easy for you to say. You're not going to have to try and explain this." When I opened the purse to put everything inside, I saw the power light for the camera was off. I wondered when the battery gave out. How much had Ian seen?

"Let me at least walk you to the door," Ray said.

"Really, that's okay," I said, but he ignored me. He also didn't bother to dress. Maybe he hoped to tempt me, and I have to admit, I felt my body react when I saw his beautiful form. My craving for him was like an addiction.

I tried to give him a quick peck on the cheek while turning away at the door, but Ray wasn't about to let me get away with that. He forcefully turned me toward him and kissed hard. His nude body pressed against me and he freely groped me. As always, his kiss took my breath away, and I gasped when his hand moved under my tank top as he thumbed my nipple. I had to get out of there and go back to my husband, but I was powerless to resist Ray, especially now that he'd had me completely.

"Ray, please. I have to go," I whined.

"Don't tell me you don't want a parting fuck, baby," he said.

"I...I...Ray..." I stammered. Although I was so sore down below, I was getting wet from his kissing and touching me. Could I handle it one more time? He unsnapped my jeans and pushed them down. I was lifted into the air and he held me with one arm while he put himself inside me. Again, no condom—again I didn't care. Did it matter now anyway? "Ohhh...Raayyyy..." I cried out.

"I knew you wanted it one more time, Em," he moaned, holding my butt as he bounced me up and down on his cock.

I leaned back against the wall with my hands on his shoulders and my legs wrapped around him. I'd always wanted to do this. It looked so sexy in movies, but it you would have to have a man as strong as Ray who could just pick you up and fuck you. My soreness was quickly forgotten as the pleasure of his cock filled me and spread throughout my body. He took me that way until my moans filled the apartment, then he let me down.

Ray's glistening cock bobbed in front of him while he turned me. With a powerful hand on my back, he bent me over the back of the couch. He entered me again and took me savagely. I cried out in both pleasure and pain while he powered inside me again and again. I loved every second of it.

"Fuck me! Fuck me, Ray!" I howled.

He pulled my hair, wrenched my head up, and I looked over my shoulder to see a huge smile on his face. "Awww, fuck, take it! Fucking take it, you little tease!"

"Yes, baby, I teased you so long. Fuck this little tease!" It had become so easy to portray the unrepentant slut. Too easy. "Come on, baby, cum for me. Cum inside me, Ray." I pleaded. I really did want to feel him cum one more time, even if I wasn't going to get there. It felt great, but I was just too sore and too used to climax anymore that night.

"Ohhh...I'm gonna cum...gonna fill you...you sexy, sexy bitch..."

Ray growled and rammed into me a final time. He was buried deep inside me as he unloaded. When he was done with me, I turned and kissed him, thrusting my tongue in his mouth. It was the best way I could thank him for an amazing night. I shimmied back into my jeans and said a final goodnight.

✳✳✳

I returned home to find Ian sitting in our den—dark except for the images on the big flat screen. There I was, pinned between Brian and Ray, and it was as dirty and sexy as any professional porn movie. I knew the receiver could record, but had hoped Ian wouldn't discover it. I didn't want my exploits recorded for posterity. I put down my bag and sat beside him on the couch. My husband didn't even look over, not even when I took his hand. It had been hours since I was performing for the camera. How many times had he watched the video?

It was the strangest feeling, watching myself. My brain could not connect what was happening on-screen with my actions just hours earlier. It was like I had walked in on Ian was just watching any old video of with anonymous porn star, not his wife—not me. I was still sore from the pounding I watched myself take on the television, but I couldn't accept it was me up there.

"Ian." He didn't answer, and I said his name again.

"Hey, hon," He spoke to me, but kept his eyes glued on the screen.

He was so preternaturally calm. It was disturbing. "Are you okay?"

"Yeah."

"Are *we* okay? Ian, talk to me." I was beginning to panic. Either he was being cold because he hated me, or his brain had short-circuited.

He finally turned to look at me, but it didn't help. I couldn't read anything in his face. "You're home late." His voice was flat. I wanted to know what I was dealing with, if he was angry, or horny, or both.

"Sorry, I fell asleep." I put on a smile, trying to be flirty. "I was pretty worn out by the end."

A smile tugged at the corner of his mouth. "I can imagine."

My frustration took over. "Ian, you're killing me. What the hell are you thinking?"

"I've got to be honest. I'm blown away. I don't know what I thought it would be like, but I wasn't expecting that."

"In a good way?" I asked tentatively.

"Yeah, I think so." He must have finally recognized the fear on my face, and said, "Emily, You love me, right? Still, I mean?"

"Of course, baby. How could you ask me that after everything…"

"Hey, don't worry, Em. I love you. I'm not angry about it, I couldn't be, could I? I mean, I asked for this, and it was the hottest thing I've ever seen. I just didn't know it would be like that."

"Do you mean when I came back with Brian?" A weight was

lifted from my shoulders. So my husband didn't want to throw me out of the house for being a slut. That was good, but he wasn't jumping on top of me the second I walked in the door either. I was afraid I'd changed the way he would look at me forever.

"Well, yeah, obviously I wasn't expecting that, but I just meant the whole thing. When you and Ray did it... the way you just gave yourself over to it... I mean—wow! You really gave yourself over."

"I thought that's what you wanted, honey. You wanted me to sleep with Ray, and I don't know any other way except to just go for it."

"No, that's not..." He paused, like he had to gather his resolve before going on. "Stop telling me you only did this for me! You wanted him! I could see it in your eyes! In the way you used your body! All this week you acted like you didn't want to do this, but... I mean, come on, Em, I'm not blind."

He didn't sound angry, but there was an accusatory edge to his voice. I guess I had that coming. I could have explained that my hesitation had nothing to do with being sexually attracted to Ray. Of course I was. Just because I'm married doesn't mean I can't find other men attractive – it just means I'm not supposed to act on those feelings. My hesitation was because I didn't want to destroy my marriage. But even though I had tried, I couldn't explain that to Ian. It was like he just couldn't comprehend the negative consequences of our doing this. So I continued to play along.

"Yes, of course I wanted to fuck Ray. He's a hot guy. I just didn't want to hurt you, honey. I was thinking about you the whole time." I squeezed his hand tighter. That was true. I had enjoyed Ray, but my husband was always there, in my mind.

"I know." His smile widened. "I saw you looking. That was... that was hot... It was like we were in it together."

"We were, honey," I said, sliding my hand to his lap. I was not surprised to find him fully hard. "It made me so wet to know you were watching me be so bad." I rubbed the lump I found in his loose pajama pants.

"I couldn't believe what I saw," he moaned.

Ian lifted his butt and let me pull his pants down. His cock sprang up and I stroked it. "I can't believe what I did tonight either. It's like I was possessed."

"It was so crazy, and so fucking sexy. You're a wonder, Emily."

"So you like seeing me all crazy and sexy?" I asked, leaning over. My hair brushed his thighs as I kissed the head of his cock. I looked back up at him.

"I did. It was unreal."

"And you liked seeing me slutty?" I asked softly, before kissing his cock again, this time lingering with my lips and sweeping the salty precum from his head with my tongue.

"Yeah...Emm..." Ian moaned when I started sucking. At first, I focused on his sensitive helmet, licking, sucking and making him quake as my hair tumbled all around my face. I could still hear the television in the background and the sounds—of flesh slapping together and my own choking moans—made me wet. I could feel my pussy tightening as I remember what it was like to have those two young studs take me. Ian surged in my mouth and I knew he truly loved watching me slut it up. I know that should have bothered me, but I loved it. I sucked my husband harder and sank down, taking all of him in my mouth.

"Uhhnn...you were so slutty, Emily...God it was hot...ohhhh soooo dirty..." Ian moaned.

I was really giving him my best blowjob, playing with his balls as I bobbed hard up and down on his cock, and I thought he would have cum quickly, especially while watching my video, but he held out. I didn't take into account that he must have been masturbating almost all night. While I was really turned on, I didn't want any more sex. I know that wasn't fair to Ian, but I was so sore, especially after fucking Ray that one, last time. But Ian, I couldn't turn him down. I'd let two other men have their way with me that night, how could I deny the same to my husband?

Ian pulled me up and kissed me while pulling at my jeans. I helped by unsnapping them, and then stood to pull them off. Ian pulled off his t-shirt and surprised me by grabbing for me, but not to throw me down on the couch. Instead, he pulled me onto his lap so I was facing away from him. This was not a position we'd ever done, but I quickly figured out what he wanted. He wanted me to watch myself on the screen while we made love. I reached between my legs for him. It hurt when he first thrust into me, and I hoped he took my groan for a moan of pleasure.

"Watch it, Emily. Watch yourself…it's so sexy…" Ian moaned to me from behind, his hands on my hips. He tilted me forward so that he could look over my shoulder and watch too.

On screen, I was on my hands and knees, taking it in both ends. It really looked like Ray and Brian were using my body, while I just tried to keep up. Ray fucked me, holding my hips, while Brian used my hair, wrapped around his fist, to pull my mouth back and forth on his cock. It was incredible to watch, and I started gushing around Ian's cock, the pain fading away. I gyrated my hips back at Ian, slowly moving on him. I still had trouble believing that was me on the television, and I couldn't take my eyes away. Ian pulled my tank top up over my breasts and reached around to play with them, pinching and pulling my nipples.

"Look at how you're taking it, Emily. It's like you were born for sex," Ian whispered.

"Yesss…" I moaned in agreement.

"Did you feel like their plaything? Did you want them to use you?"

I knew what Ian wanted to hear, and it was easy to tell him, because it was the truth. "Yes, honey. I wanted them to use me all night. I wanted you to see them use me. Ohhh…Ian…"

"I love this part," he told me, thrusting up to meet me as I came down on him.

I watched Ray turn me onto my side, and then I saw myself obey Brian's command when he told me to beg for his cock. Ray slammed me from behind, and once I'd begged, I had a mouthful of cock again. God, I was such a slut. So this was Ian's favorite part? Interesting. I bounced harder and harder on Ian's cock as I rubbed my juicy clit. I hadn't thought it was possible, but Ian was going to make me cum.

"Fuck me…fuck your little slut…ohhh…*Ian*…" I begged my husband. My eyes were fixed on the screen and I knew his were too.

"God you're a slut…such a fucking slut…" Ian grunted.

"Yesss…yessss…I'm your slut…fuck meeee…fuck meeee… *Ian…cum with me…*"

Ian and I were both consumed and captivated by my video, but also totally locked into each other. I was performing for him again, and I wanted to make him proud. And God, did I want to cum! We both did, crying out. I gushed around my husband's cock while he came deep inside me. When we were finished, I reached for the remote, turned off the television and fell back against him.

"Can we please go to bed now?" I begged, exhausted.

EPILOGUE

THE NEXT MORNING, over coffee, we finally had a real talk. We slept late, but still had an hour before we had to go pick up the kids. Ian wanted to make love in the morning, but I begged off. I was so sore at that point, I didn't know if I'd ever have sex again. Once I was dressed and comfortable, I made coffee and toasted some bagels. We sat across the table from each other.

"So, about last night…" I started.

" Yeah... last night...," Ian sounded drained.

"Are we okay?" I asked

"You still love me?"

"Of course I do. More than ever," I reassured him.

"Then we're good." His tone spoke volumes that his words didn't.

"If you have something to say, Ian, just say it."

"I'm…" he paused. "Last night was incredible, but I don't think I could take another like it."

I couldn't believe his nerve. Ian kicked all of this into motion and now he made it sound like I'd put *him* through some kind of ordeal? Unreal. "Let me get this straight. You're telling me that you enjoyed watching me act like a... well, like a complete slut last night..."

"Yes."

"...that you're not mad about it..."

"I'm not."

"...that you still love me..."

"More than ever."

"...and now your fantasy has been fulfilled?"

"I think so, yeah."

"You think so? I hope so. Because like I said Friday, that's it for me. It was an amazing night, but my fantasies have been fulfilled too. I don't need to go back there again."

"Neither do I." He clasped my hands in his. "I love you, Em. I was so afraid I'd lost you."

"What are you going to say to Ray tomorrow at work?"

"I've been thinking about that. I have the time, so I'm taking the week off. I'm going to tell my boss I hurt myself over the weekend and I can't come in."

Ian looked surprised. "Do you really want to do that? Shouldn't you have some closure?"

"I've had all the closure I need with Ray," I said with a smile. "It's best this way."

"Good," he said.

"I know, I'm just saying I don't need any more closure with Ray. I'd really rather just not see him again."

I didn't want to tell my husband the real reason I didn't want to see Ray again. What I couldn't tell Ian was that I was scared of my attraction to Ray. He was more than just a plaything with to me. Not only was Ray very sexy, but he also funny and smart, and I loved his carefree attitude. Deep down, I knew that now that I had given myself to him, I would be powerless to resist Ray. I didn't want to give myself that way to any man other than my husband. It just wasn't right. If I went back to work, I knew Ray would push, and we would end up fucking every day. I couldn't put myself in that position. Maybe Ian was okay sharing me and my body with Ray. But he didn't know that it had become more than *just sex* for me. I could never share my heart with another man.

"I'm surprised you can just walk away now. Just days ago, all you could think about was me fucking another man. Now you're totally done with that? What happened?"

"Just started to feel like this was becoming less about us and more about you and Ray..."

"But it's always been about us."

"And I realized that..."

"That we might be turning into one of *those* couples?" Emily finished.

"*Those* couples?"

"You know, bringing other men into the bedroom. Or, I don't know, swinging or whatever," I said.

"My point is that I was afraid that things went too far to fix."

"Our marriage isn't like a broken TV. It's not something that can be easily fixed," I replied. "But it's not broken either. At least, I don't think so."

"Me neither."

He leaned across the table and kissed me hard. "I love you too, Emily, and I would never want to do anything that would risk our family. If I lost you, I would lose my mind. You're everything to me."

"And you are to me. I love you and our family with all my heart. Now let's go get the kids and be together as a family."

That was the last time Ian and I ever spoke about that night in detail. Sure, we relived it plenty of times, but as time passed, it happened less and less. Ian seemed to have sated his darker desires, and was happy to go back to our marriage as if nothing had happened.

I say *seemed*, because some things did change. He encouraged me to dress sexily when we went out. Some of his suggestions bordered on the slutty, but I didn't mind, because I could finally admit that I liked the attention.

Oddly, I was the one who couldn't quite put everything to bed, so to speak. Ray never totally disappeared from my thoughts. Occasionally, when I found myself home alone, I pulled out that video and watched it while I gave myself an intense orgasm. I still couldn't believe I was the woman in the video with Ray and Brian. The darkest parts of me wanted to be that woman again, like when I saw a good looking guy at the gym, or out on the street. It was so exciting to be the woman who gave her lover blowjobs in the front seat of the car. But I could never be her again—I had too much to lose.

Still, it was hard to give up, and I fear I haven't given it up completely. Rather than make sure I'm not giving a peek down my blouse, I *make sure* I do when I'm in the mood. When I'm out and about, I flirt with men more than I ever did before, and I enjoy their attention. I do it for Ian's benefit sometimes when we're out on a date night, but I do it when he's not there, too. The thrill I get from the attention of other men is electric. I began to wonder if I would ever cross the line again—despite what Ian and I had promised each other. I could not discuss these things with my husband, though. He sounded pretty final when he said he never wanted to play like that again, and I truly did not want to risk losing what we'd worked so hard to build together. But I was so full of conflicting feelings. I began a journal shortly thereafter, hoping to make sense of my confusing, conflicting feelings. It was the one place I could be fully honest with myself about my fantasies and feelings. And I hoped that would be enough. I didn't *know* that I wanted to play again, I just wasn't sure that I could just turn off what had been turned on inside me.

AFTERWARD

The idea for this book started when, Kenny Wright shared the beginning of a new project he was working on. It was the story of a man who gets hot by the idea of seeing his wife have sex with another man and decides to do something about it. A chance meeting with one of her younger, attractive coworkers sets that husband—Ian—on a course that would, indeed, lead his wife into the arms of this other man. I was intrigued by this story, written entirely from Ian's point-of-view, and told Kenny that I wondered what exactly was going through the wife's—Emily—mind when Ian told her he wanted her to be with other men. How would an ordinary woman react to that? I wasn't thinking in terms of the typical female lead in an erotic story, who's generally pretty happy to go along with this sort of thing, but how would a woman who'd never considered such a thing react? It helped that Emily was already attracted to her coworker, Ray. Happily, Kenny encouraged me to write Emily's story. We would figure out how to integrate everything later.

We agreed early on that Emily must never find out about Ian pushing Ray towards her, because she would see that as a manipulation and find it hard to get past. But as the story progressed, we began to differ on the direction and who these people really were. We decided at that time that we would present this project as two different stories. Kenny struggled with the direction Ian's character seemed to be taking, and I had strong feelings about who Emily was and how she would react to all of this. We finished what would become *Because*

He's Watching, but Kenny was not ready to put Ian's side out there. He had to reflect on it I had no such reservations, and thus published *Because He's Watching* to some success in the summer of 2011.

In late 2013, Kenny revisited Ian and came up with a new way to tackle the character. What he finished is certainly a stronger, deeper character study of a man with an obsession. I think it's some of Kenny's best work, though I may not be objective. *Because He's Watching: Ian's Obsession* was published in December 2013 and available at most online ebook retailers.

During our renewed discussions of what the future held for Ian and Emily, Kenny and I also decided that their story wasn't over. Could they really go through such an intense experience and then just let it go? Some doors cannot be closed. We've began discussing how to continue this couple's story and hopefully we will have something out there this year—this time a combined tale.

Kenny isn't the only one I have to acknowledge here. As always, I have to thank my kind, patient husband who allows me to find time to write, which is not the easiest thing with two small children running around! And I'm lucky to have a man who indulges and encourages my kinkier side. I also want to thank my friend Julie for her editing. Without her help, this would not be the story it is. Any remaining errors are mine, of course. And thank you to all of you who have read this book in the last couple years and reviewed it at Amazon and sent your words of encouragement. They mean more to me than you'll ever know.

KM
8 January 2014

Excerpt from

Because He's Watching: Ian's Obsession
by Kenny Wright

ONE

THE CRACK OF colliding pool balls and the pleasant murmur of conversation were my first impressions of Bar 88. It was early still and the sparse crowd of after work businessmen and women looked like a beer commercial ready to happen. I got the feeling that it was only waiting for the six o'clock hour.

I settled in at the bar and ordered a beer, despite the long list of happy hour cocktails and the towering display of top shelf liquor. This was as good a place as any to grab a drink, and after today's fruitless meetings, I needed one or two.

The ambiance was upscale. Bar 88 was the type of suburban neighborhood bar that the yuppies hung out at. A handful of pool tables were sprinkled throughout the lower level while the upper floor, high in the unfinished rafters, was more of a dining area that overlooked the bar. It looked empty, although again, it was early.

Two of the billiard tables were occupied, one by a rowdy group of college guys, the other by a solitary player who looked like another escapee from the office. Like me, he wore the remains of the workday like scraps of armor: trousers that had picked up wrinkles, a tie-less and fitted oxford with the shirt-sleeves rolled up his forearms, a Blackberry clipped to his belt.

He was about ten years younger, maybe in his late twenties or early thirties, and built in a way I never was. His thick arms bulged under his rolled sleeves and his barrel chest spoke of time spent in the gym. A military crew-cut completed his look and while he did not look at all like someone I would hang out with, I just couldn't shake the feeling that I knew him. He was shooting alone, working the table with determined focus, and based on the number of scratches and missed shots, he was in the early stages of learning the game.

It took half my beer to place him. I couldn't recall his name, but I was pretty sure he worked with my wife, Emily. That was it. I'd seen him in a couple of photographs she'd shown me from office events and I seemed to recall him being introduced as one of the new employees at the last Christmas party.

I decided to join him. I still had a few hours to kill due my disaster of a meeting. I hadn't played pool in forever and it seemed like a good idea at the time. Little did I know...

"Hey there," I said as I walked up to his table.

The man turned to me, the pool stick by his side, and stared at me without recognition. "Hey," he replied after a beat.

Okay, so he didn't recognize me, but that was fair since I still didn't remember his name. I made a snap decision to chat with him, figuring I might learn some embarrassing stories about my wife I could use to tease her later. It's not every day you get an insight into what your other half is like when you're not around.

"You're not bad. Want to split a few games?" I asked.

It must have come off as oddly forward from a stranger. I could see the wheels turning as he tried to figure out if I was trying to pick him up or hustle him. He must have decided to trust me because he shrugged and said, "Why not? Want to play for who pays?" He had a crisp voice, though not as deep as I'd expected.

"Perfect." I set my beer down and picked out a pool cue.

"I'm Ray," he offered as he racked the balls. "I haven't seen you around here..."

Still didn't remember me and an idea flashed through my mind.

"Neil," I greeted, exchanging a hard handshake. For the life of me, I have no idea where that came from, or why I did it. I told myself I would get better stories about Emily if he didn't know I was her husband. This first lie started me down a slippery slope.

Ray was about three inches taller and had an easy, quick smile that I imagined women responded well to. He was handsome in that generic, all-American way.

"Actually, this is my first time here. Was in the neighborhood for a meeting and, well, we were thrown out. The others decided to take the day off and go home, but it was my project. I need a drink."

"Sorry to hear that. Why don't I get the first round?"

I set the racked balls on the green felt and smirked. "What makes you think you won't be anyway, when I beat you?"

"Fair enough." Again, that grin.

We shot around a little and neither of us was very good. We chit-chatted while we played and I had the oddest feeling, like I was playing with fire. What did I really think I would hear about my Emily? I asked if this was his usual haunt.

"Yeah, I come here pretty often. I've recently gotten into pool, and there's usually a table open on the weekdays. It's not a bad place and the Happy Hour prices are pretty reasonable, despite the neighborhood."

A pretty brunette barmaid in her early twenties passed by, wearing a short, cut-off jean skirt and a halter top that did little to hide her full breasts. "Nice staff, too," I commented as I watched her put in an order at the bar.

Ray gave a chuckle. "There's that, too, although she's a little young for me."

"Like them older?"

Ray laughed again, taking his turn to sink a few balls. "You know, sometimes a little experience can go a long way."

We talked about the neighborhood and what we did for work. Other than the bit about my name, I kept things truthful. I was an architect in the city. I had two kids, was married for close to ten years. Ray told me he worked as a technical writer at TNK, where Emily also works, and was single, with no girlfriend or kids and had a place in the city. He liked his life and wasn't ready to settle down quite yet, but it did seem like he felt he was lagging behind his peers.

"There was a phase when all my friends were getting married. I went to a wedding every month, it seemed. Now, it's baby showers," he said

"I remember those days."

"Not for me. Not yet, anyway. I'm still having fun."

"The crazy life of a single, young technical writer," I joked. "Probably not much eye-candy at work. I can see why you need to unwind here."

My wife was one of only two women in her department who wasn't an administrative assistant.

"You'd be surprised."

"Yeah?" I asked. "Is there a lot of ass over there at TNK? I've got a buddy who works IT for you guys and he always talks about the women he sees when he needs to come up and fix something." I figured it was a safe lie, since in my experience most IT guys get ignored.

"There are a few, actually."

"Oh yeah? Who's the hottest chick in your office?"

I couldn't believe I was going down this road. The plan was to find out something embarrassing about Emily, not find out if the guys in her office had the hots for her. I didn't stop him, though. It would be kind of exciting to hear some other guy talk about my wife the way guys do.

Ray didn't even hesitate. "One of them puts apple-cheeks over there to shame."

"Now I'm intrigued..." I didn't dare think ahead. Not one second.

"You should be!" Ray shot a ball into the corner pocket with force. "Light eyes and dark hair. Nice body. A real natural beauty. God, I love that look."

"Me too." My stomach fluttered. I could barely trust myself to speak. Emily. He had to be talking about Emily.

He didn't stop. I didn't stop him. "She's got a body to match. About five-five or so, with the perkiest set of tits." He held his hands out as though grasping Emily's full B-cups. "She works out every day at lunch at a gym around the corner from the office. Hell, I started doing the same, just to watch her sweat in those tight little outfits of hers. If I've ever seen a more perfect ass..." He shook his head.

I'd gone fishing for compliments for my wife and pulled up a whale. I was happy to be fortified by alcohol or this would have been difficult. I should have been offended to hear him talk about my wife that way, right? Unfortunately, the alcohol also made it impossible to keep myself from digging deeper.

"You ever hit that?"

Why the hell did I ask that? Emily would never cheat on me! How did I keep my voice so even when I felt like such a mess? I held the pool cue with both hands to keep them from shaking.

Ray laughed, shaking his head. "Nah. I mean, we flirt, but nothing beyond that. She's married."

"Don't tell me that's stopped you in the past." What the hell was I saying?

"Hey, I respect the institution of marriage…most of the time." He leaned on his pool cue, grinning wide. "Sometimes, when we're talking, dude, all I can think about is her riding me, that tight little body of hers bouncing up and down on me… But anyway, if there's one thing I'm going to regret when I move, it's probably that chick."

"Oh? You moving?"

"In two weeks. Up to Philly."

I licked my lips. I spoke before I could stop myself. "Then you've got nothing to lose. In two weeks, you'll be gone. I say go for it."

"You may have point," he said.

Oh God, was I really doing this? Was I really talking this guy into going after my wife? My mouth kept opening and closing, and words kept pouring out.

"How long has she been married? You know?"

"Forever and a day, I think. Couple kids, too."

"Well, then there's probably not much excitement left there. It's probably all sex once a month and only in the dark."

Ray shrugged. "I doubt that. She's still hot after two kids and any woman who keeps herself in shape like that is a goer." He finished his beer and signaled for another pitcher. "Emily's wild under that conservative exterior. C'mon, you know the type."

Hearing Ray say her name was like a slap to the face. There was no doubt about it now. He was talking about my wife. And he did seem to have a real line on what she's like. My darker side charged full bore ahead.

"Sure. So you think she's like that?"

I'd gone digging. Was a prepared for what I found? Emily had always been the ultimate girl-next-door: warm and charming and pretty, proper and well behaved. That Ray thought differently was a shock—although a very stimulating one.

"I know women. She has all the signs."

The signs? What signs?

"It's just the way she presents herself. She wears these tailored business suits, right? Always looks professional, with the perfect hair and make-up. But underneath, well… Let's just say I've caught glimpses of the woman beneath the suit. Sometimes there's the line of her thong under a tight skirt, or the lacy top of a stocking, or if I'm really lucky she leans forward just a little too far and you can see down her blouse. I'm not the only one who's noticed, believe me. We're always on the lookout for a piece."

Emily did enjoy sexy lingerie, although I had to admit it had been a long time since I'd paid much attention to it. The stockings were a bit of a surprise though, since she'd always complained whenever I'd asked her to wear them for me, even though I know wearing them made her feel sexy.

"And then there were the few times she's gone out to happy hour with us," Ray went on. "The business exterior melts. She undoes a couple of those buttons on her blouse and really loosens up. You know what I mean."

Did I? "Sounds like an interesting lady."

Ray nodded. "You've got that right. She's been in a relationship so long that maybe she's forgotten what getting all hot and heavy is like. All women like to be swept off their feet, you know, get caught up in the moment and throw caution to the wind."

"Has she?" I croaked and sipped my beer. "I mean, thrown caution to the wind?"

"Not yet, but I think I see it there, the gleam in her eye, that she wants to. Maybe she just needs a little push," he said thoughtfully.

"And maybe you're the one to push her," I said.

Oh God, what had I done?

Even as half of me freaked out at what I'd just done, the other half rationalized that he had to be wrong. He had to be projecting, seeing what he wanted to see because he wanted to screw her.

"I'd better hit the road, it being a school night and all."

"Yeah, I need to get out of here too," Ray agreed. We shook. "I usually shoot on my own, but it was fun hanging out and having some guy talk."

"Yeah, it was. Maybe I'll see you around. You can tell me more about this piece of ass Emily."

"Yeah, that'd be cool. Hopefully next time, I'll have something to share. I'm usually here after work. Stop by anytime."

TWO

I GOT IN my car—a bad idea, considering the amount I'd had to drink—and drove home. It was the least reckless thing I'd done so far, I figured, and if I died, who cared?

Reviewing the facts drunkenly, I concluded that this had definitely been a fun little exercise. There was no real harm done, after all. Emily was a loving wife as always, and my own sense of pride was stroked by listening to a stranger talk about how attractive she was.

Then my mind flashed to some of things Ray actually said. *One of them puts apple-cheeks over there to shame...Watching her ride me...*

I'd been here before. No use denying the drunken mind.

A year ago.

At my nephew's wedding.

I'd watched Emily dance with some of the groomsmen, all about Ray's age, all handsome in their youth. When Emily had spotted me watching her, she'd returned, shyly, and asked if I was upset with her. I wasn't. More than that, I was strangely turned on by it. I'd blown out my knee and couldn't dance, so I'd encouraged her to have fun.

Throughout the night, she floated from one set of arms to another. As time went on and the drinks continued to flow, I noticed that she kept going to one guy in particular. Watching from the outside, I noticed the unspoken pact among the men. This guy had laid claim to her and the others knew to back off. Emily was naive. I wasn't.

The craziest thing was that I wasn't upset. I felt jealous, sure. A little flattered that a younger man would show that kind of attention to my beautiful wife. And pretty fucking turned on. All at the same time.

Nothing ended up happening other than some questionably inappropriate touching on the dance floor. Emily was diligent about moving his hands north, although her resolve seemed to break down toward the end of the evening, particularly during the slower songs. I'll never forget the image of her dancing in his arms, head resting on his shoulder, eyes closed.

That night, we had wild, newlywed sex. I think we were both a little surprised at how turned on we were by the evening. We never talked about what had us both so turned on that night. It was like it never happened, except for the teasing asides Emily would give me when I'd catch her talking to another man—even in innocent, mixed company.

By the time I pulled into my driveway after Bar 88, I was a little sobered up and a lot turned on. Of course, it was neither of these things that my wife noticed when I walked into the bedroom.

"Did you drive home like that?" she asked sharply.

"Like what?" Best defense: play ignorant.

"You're drunk," Emily said, putting her hands on her hips, the dark arches of her eyebrows shooting up.

"And you're sexy..."

She tilted her head to her side, her tussled dark locks spilling across her shoulder. She tried to maintain her stern expression, but her hazel eyes gave her away. We'd been best friends for years and I always knew how to get myself out of trouble. "You think some sweet words'll get you off the hook?"

"They're not just words!" I protested. I checked her out like a teenager. She was ready for bed. Her little boy-shorts and camisole didn't cover much of her body, lean and tight. Since having the kids, she'd always sported a little belly—nothing pronounced, just a softness around the edges she didn't have when she was younger. For the first time, I realized that that softness was gone, along with the little pooch. How long ago had she lost that?

I felt my cock rise, seeing her as Ray did: as a woman he wanted to bed. I reached out and touched her neck, running my thumb along the smooth skin of her jaw. She nuzzled into my touch.

I stepped even closer, forcing her to look at me with those luminous eyes. When we kissed, I imagined Ray kissing her. My cock grew even harder. I felt her breasts compress between us, felt the exposed flesh between her small top and even smaller bottoms. I pushed my tongue past her lips and we kissed like we hadn't in a long, long time.

"The kids in bed?" I asked as we separated.

Emily nodded, looking up at me.

"Come on..."

I couldn't blame Ray for admiring Emily's ass. It was nicely padded with a firm tuck before tapering into her taut thighs. Catching up to her, I slid my hand down the back of her boy-shorts and squeezed.

"Ian." She giggled, rolling her eyes. We kissed again.

I finally let my drunk brain catch up, pawing her tits until I felt her nipples harden under my palms. As she peeled her cami top over her head, I watched her as though it was Ray watching her, and everything felt new. She released her breasts with a healthy wobble. Her nipples were elongated, casting short shadows across the pale swells.

When she shimmied out of her boy-shorts, I guided her to the bed before sinking to my knees. Her lightly freckled skin glowed as I placed kisses along the slopes of her tits, finding each pink nipple and swirling it. Her tips were incredibly sensitive, so I moved on quickly, saving that treat for later.

Squeezing the soft tit-flesh together, I rolled her nubs with my thumbs as my mouth worked lower. Down her stomach. Across her navel. I pushed her onto her back as I kissed across the trimmed wedge of pubic hair she kept above her pussy. I followed it down to her clit, eliciting a shiver and a moan as I passed quickly over it and on to smoother, wetter skin.

I glanced up along her body as I began to work her. She'd propped herself up on her elbows, but her head was lolled back and to the side.

"Oh... yes..."

What Ray wouldn't give to be in my position? To slice his tongue along her slit. To feel her shaved folds along his lips. Drilling a couple fingers deep within her, I twisted and curled in exactly the way I knew she loved.

"Ah! AH!" she cried, remembering to muffle herself at the last second or wake the kids.

I crawled up her body before she could fully recover, pulling off my pants and boxers in the process. Kissing the exposed ivory skin of her neck, I lined myself up and eased into her juicy sex. She was snug but welcoming. She wrapped a hand around my neck as we were united.

Again, I thought of Ray's words, coming at me through the fog of my drunkenness.

Watching her ride me...

That tight body of hers bouncing and covered in sweat...

"Let's turn," I whispered after a few more long and frantic strokes. Emily groaned, but didn't protest beyond that. Riding me was one of her favorite positions.

We reformed at the head of the bed with me reclined on a stack of pillows and Emily easing herself into my lap. I watched her bounce as I collected her tits in my palms and kneaded them gently. Worked her. Got her ready.

"Oh, Ian..." Emily sighed as my lips swallowed her left nipple. I prodded it with the tip of my tongue, feeling her pussy cave around me. She cradled my head against her bosom, using it as leverage to fuck me. I switched nipples, treating the right with the same knowing attention as its twin. Her breath grew shallower. Her sighs took on a reedy, thin sound.

Her voice broke. "Oh... Ian..."

We kissed when she couldn't take it anymore. I slid my hands down her backside, cupping the hard cheeks of her buttocks. I helped her bounce harder. Faster. I could feel her hard nips graze my chest, feel our sweat mix and glide between us. *That tight body of hers bouncing and covered in sweat...*

I attacked her neck, knowing how sensitive she was there. I

could taste the salt of her perspiration. Could feel the vibrations of her moans beneath my lips. It spurred me on. I fucked her harder. Faster. She leaned into me, her thighs tightening as she rutted.

She was close. I was close. More sweat collected between our bodies and our skin slithered. She arched back, presenting her wondrous breasts to me. To Ray. To her illicit lover. I saw him holding her, his muscular arms strained. She raked her fingers along her scalp, where the dark locks had begun to clump and cling in their dampness.

"Huhh!" she cried, cumming. "Oh, Ian!"

She climaxed, reaching her oblivion as I smashed through my own. "Cum, Ian! Cum now! Please!"

I clawed down her back. Feeling the dimples above her buttocks. Feeling that ass, wanted by so many. I came, eyes closed, out of breath. I came with a force that caught me by surprise. That drained me.

The night snuck up on me at last. The booze. The talk. The discoveries. Here's where I should have come clean. Should have talked about these tumultuous emotions inside of me. We could have done the Best Friend thing and worked through it. Instead, I chose to close my eyes and let sleep take me.

I watched her pad naked into the bathroom. I crawled up under the sheets. Sleep was not far behind.

ABOUT THE AUTHOR

Kirsten McCurran lives in the suburbs with her husband, young children and a dog named Jake. She lives out her vivid fantasy life through her writing. Kirsten is most interested in exploring the fantasies and inner sexual lives of women like her. The more she writes, the crazier her fantasies become and she's just as excited to see what she comes up with next as she hopes you are. Kirsten is the author of over 20 ebooks. She would love to hear feedback on her work and can be reached at kmccurran@gmail.com Goodreads or through Twitter @ kirstenmccurran.